A GENTLEMAN FOR CHRISTMAS

by
PRESCOTT LANE

Copyright © 2018 Prescott Lane
Print Edition

Cover design © Michele Catalano Creative
Cover image from Shutterstock by AS Inc
Editing by Nikki Rushbrook

This is a work of fiction. All characters, organizations, and events portrayed in this novel are either products of the author's imagination or used fictitiously. All rights reserved. This book or any portion thereof may not be reproduced or used in any manner whatsoever without the express written permission of the author, except for the use of brief quotations in a book review.

TABLE OF CONTENTS

Prologue	1
Chapter One	3
Chapter Two	7
Chapter Three	17
Chapter Four	29
Chapter Five	38
Chapter Six	46
Chapter Seven	51
Chapter Eight	58
Chapter Nine	64
Chapter Ten	74
Chapter Eleven	80
Chapter Twelve	90
Chapter Thirteen	96
Chapter Fourteen	104
Chapter Fifteen	111
Chapter Sixteen	118
Chapter Seventeen	121
Epilogue	125
Also by Prescott Lane	128
Acknowledgements	129
About the Author	130

PROLOGUE

JAX

"Thou shalt not covet thy neighbor's wife."

Otherwise known as the original bros before hoes commandment.

I'm not advocating calling women hoes. It's an expression, so put away your Encyclopedia of Political Correctness.

There are rules in life. The Ten Commandments were just the beginning. We have rules for everything. How to drive. How to dress. How to walk across the fucking street. So why not rules for love? That's how all this started—a set of rules between my buddies and me.

The Bro Code.

Obviously, bros before hoes is rule one. We vowed never to let a girl come between us, which meant if one of us liked a girl, she was forever off limits.

Little did I know our teenage pact would launch my multi-million dollar career. A little tweaking here and some socially acceptable rewording there and The Gentleman's Handbook was born.

I've written books and given seminars on everything from how to find love, to how to propose, to how to have a successful long-distance relationship. You name it, and I've got rules for it. Personally, I've never been much of a rule follower, but that's my little secret.

The funny thing is I've never been in love. Well, there is this one girl, but we won't talk about her. It does no good to think about someone you can't have and never will.

My lack of emotional commitment hasn't slowed down my career one bit. Currently, I have two books on the New York Times Best Sellers List. My seminars sell out like a Drake concert.

I always find it interesting that the rules started between a group of male friends, but it's mostly women that come to hear me speak. Occasionally, you see the poor sap boyfriend who was dragged along to listen, but for the most part it's all women.

This time of the year is no exception. December first until January first is important for guys. Holidays are big for a lot of couples. If you don't know what you're doing for your lady, you better figure it out and fast. In fact, my rule is that you should be paying attention all year long.

Trust me on this. If you remember something she mentioned she liked three months ago and surprise her with it at Christmas, she'll spread her legs before Santa even has time to slide down the chimney. Let's be honest, that is always at least part of the goal for guys.

So my current work in progress tackles Christmas. A how-to guide for the holidays.

The Gentleman's Rules for Christmas.

CHAPTER ONE

JAX

How can something that feels so right at night feel so wrong the next morning?

I broke my own rule. Sleeping with an ex is never a good idea. Don't give me any of that closure bullshit. You break up with someone for a reason. Going back for one more round between the sheets isn't going to help anyone move on. And last night was round twelve or so for us.

Fuck me!

We broke up over a year ago, but once a month or so she calls me under the guise of needing to talk, some broken appliance, needing a man for something and before you know it, I have her pinned against the wall, pounding my dick inside of her. That's what she needs a man for.

I don't stay the night. We don't talk about getting back together. It's just sex, but I know it's the reason that she hasn't moved on. I know she thinks that we will get back together, so I'm not doing her any favors by continuing to sleep with her. I have to cut this off. Last night at her place, that was it.

I stare up at my ceiling, thankful that at least we aren't having the awkward morning after. I came home. I've got some serious sexual remorse going on. Like I said, it felt good at the time, but not so much right now.

I'm not an asshole. Well, I try not to be, but this is an asshole thing I'm doing. Time to go cold turkey—at least with her. It will only take me saying I can't come over one time for her to get the message. It doesn't need to be a big thing, so next time she calls I won't go over there. It's time I follow my own rules.

Gentleman's Rule—Don't fuck an ex unless you want to fuck them up.

I roll out of my bed, pulling on some shorts and hitting the button on the remote control to raise the window shades, the Gulf of Mexico calling me. I've lived in Waterscape, Florida, my whole life, but just bought my place on the beach last month.

Growing up, I dreamed of owning a place like this. When I was a kid, I lived several miles inland in a duplex with my mom. It was nice, but nothing like waking up to the water every day. I bought this place over a year ago, but it's taken that long to make it livable. For all the time and money I put into it, I could've built a new house, but there's something special about this spot. Hanging out with my friends and looking down the beach at this place, I made a promise that one day I'd own it, and now I do. I own it outright. No mortgage on this baby.

I've got no excuse for the lack of furniture, though, except that I've only lived here a month. My bedroom, the living room, and home gym are the only rooms furnished. What more does a man really need? The rest of the rooms are bare. The dining room has a rug, but that's it. The pool has one lounge chair beside it. It's all a work in progress.

I press another button on the remote, opening the windows, letting the gulf breeze in. Even though it's less than a week before Christmas, it's not cold here. There's a crispness to the air, but we won't be getting any blizzards. There might be some surfing Santas, but they'll be in board shorts, not Santa suits.

My cell phone vibrates on the nightstand, and I say a silent prayer that I'm not being put to the test with my ex already. A relieved smile comes to my face when I see it's a different woman, Maci, one of my closest friends and married to my other friend, Malcolm.

There was a crew of five of us that have all hung out since we were little. Maci and Malcolm started dating by the time they were pre-teens and have been together ever since. They got married right out of college and have twins, a boy and a girl.

"Jax, oh thank God you answered," Maci says in the panicked tone that only a young mother can have. "The twins have the stomach flu. They've been sick all night. It's coming out of both ends."

"Okay, I got it," I say, trying to erase that image from my mind.

"Let me talk to him," I hear Malcolm say in the background. There's some shuffling noise and then Malcolm's on the line. "It's chaos over here, man."

"Uncle Jax's duties do not include bodily fluids," I tease, but he knows damn well I'd clean his kids' shit up for him if he needed me to.

"Maci and I got that. It's . . ." he pauses. "Luke and Skylar."

Luke and Skylar round out our quintuplet of friendship. Growing up, Skylar and I lived next to each other in the duplex. We shared a bedroom wall until we both went off to college. We shared a lot more than that. Skylar and I had the closest friendship of all of us until I fucked it up. She and Luke went to prom together, and he followed her off to college. They've been dating ever since, about ten years now.

"Skylar broke up with him," Malcolm says. "Apparently, he . . ."

"Malcolm!" Maci yells in the background.

"Daddy duty calls," he says. "I'm giving the phone back to Maci."

Skylar and Luke broke up? The only couple I know that's been together longer than them are Malcolm and Maci, and of course, they're married, and Skylar and Luke aren't. But still, it's been ten years!

Skylar's single? That shouldn't make my heart jump. As my friend's ex-girlfriend, she's still off limits to me.

"I need you to get Skylar from the airport," Maci says, breathless. "I was supposed to drive to Pensacola myself, but I can't leave Malcolm with two sick kids. Can you do it?"

"She's coming today? I thought she and Luke were coming for

New Years?"

"Change of plans," Maci says. I hear her draw a deep breath. "Skylar broke up with Luke a few weeks ago, on her birthday. She didn't want me to say anything to anyone. I didn't even tell Malcolm."

"Luke didn't tell me," I say. "I haven't heard from him in a month or so."

"It's bad," Maci says. "But you know Skylar. She was trying to muscle on like a good little soldier."

Yep, that's the Skylar I know. Sweet, smart, sassy, not to mention sexy as hell, but in a pure, wholesome way—long brown hair, big blue eyes, pale skin with the most kissable lips you've ever seen and that one dimple on her right cheek that pops out when she smiles.

"I finally convinced her to come home. Spend Christmas here," Maci says. "But now the kids are sick. We were in the emergency room all night. Could you please pick her up this afternoon?"

"Text me her flight information," I say. "I got her."

Hanging up, I stare at my phone. *I got her.* If only that were true. She's the one girl I don't have. The one girl I can never have.

Bros before hoes.

CHAPTER TWO

SKYLAR

JUST MAKE IT to Maci. Just make it to Maci. Then you can have a good, old-fashioned cry with your best girlfriend. I must repeat that to myself a thousand times on my flight from Chicago to Florida. I wasn't planning on coming home for Christmas. I wasn't supposed to be home until New Years. No one but Malcolm and Maci know I'm coming now. I'll call my mom when I land. Everything happened so fast that all I could think about was getting out of the city. As soon as the plane touches down, I feel the tears welling in my eyes, knowing Maci is waiting to greet me with open arms.

It's only been a few months since I've seen her, but there's nothing like good friends when times are tough. Maci is the best. She's not only my friend, but she and I have a small business together—a handmade natural soap company we named after me, since Maci joked about already having a big company named after her. We are in a few small boutique stores. I handle branding and publicity, she oversees our small manufacturing operation in Florida, and we work together on the creative aspects. It's difficult to manage sometimes since we don't live in the same city, so every few months, I travel to Florida for business. I wish this trip was for business, but it's not. It's for heartbreak.

The plane reaches the gate, and everyone leaps up from their seats like it's a race. From the look of the overhead compartments filled with gifts wrapped in various Christmas paper, they're probably all traveling for the holidays.

I wait for a break in line then stand up, reaching to get my carry-on bag. At five feet five inches, I'm not tall, but I'm not short. Still, getting the bag down from over my head isn't easy. There are two men in front of me, and three behind me, and not one offers to help when they see me struggling, instead looking more annoyed that it's taking me so long. They'll be waiting for a cold day in hell if they're waiting for me to apologize for my lack of upper body strength.

Usually the first thing I do after a flight is use the airport bathroom, but today I head straight through the terminal. I don't need to catch a glimpse of myself in any mirrors, knowing my eyes are still puffy, and my hair is still in a messy bun and not in the cute way.

I told Maci not to park and come in, just to meet me outside baggage claim, which was stupid because all I brought is one carry-on, and I'm not even sure what's inside. I was in such a state when I packed it. I hate this. I'm not this girl. I was doing fine with the breakup. I really was, trucking on like I always do, not missing a beat. I was the picture-perfect version of a healthy, newly single gal, until last night. Freaking last night.

Pulling out my phone, I turn off airplane mode, waiting for it to come back to life. Luke has been blowing up my phone, so I should leave it off, but I need to check to see if Maci has messaged me that she's running late or anything. The thing starts dinging like a pissed off alarm clock, and I frantically reach for the vibrate button.

Blowing out a deep breath, I look up, right into his deep blue eyes. My legs stop. Someone bumps into me from behind. He flashes me the smile that I know so well. The one I saw every day growing up. I don't want to cry in front of him. Not him. What's he doing here?

His smile slowly fades, and I realize I'm standing right at the security line. The one with the ominous message that reads once you cross it, there's no going back. How appropriate!

He stands there for a second in his jeans, white t-shirt, and brown leather jacket, holding a bouquet of flowers. If this were a movie, this would be the scene where the girl runs to her man in the airport, leaps in his arms, and they kiss as he twirls her around. The problem with that is I'm not his girl, and he's not my man. We used to be best friends. Now, not so much.

Instead, I take a step back and throw up all over my favorite winter boots. They're waterproof and made for the snow. Wonder if they can withstand vomit, too?

That's when the tears come. I don't know about you, but throwing up and crying go hand in hand for me. I'm tired, embarrassed, mortified that some airport worker is going to have to clean up my bodily fluids, horrified that other travelers now must side-step the contents of my stomach. If there was ever a time to crawl into a hole, it's now. I hear the security guy yelling and look up, finding Jax marching right toward me.

"Arrest me," Jax yells at the poor TSA guy as he crosses the line of doom. The man who writes about rules doesn't like to follow them. "I got you," he whispers to me, handing me the flowers then bending down, braving my vomit. He unties my boots and slips them off my feet. "You really know how to say hello to a guy," he says, giving me a little wink.

"Sir, this is your last warning," the TSA guy yells.

Jax rolls his eyes, placing his hand at the small of my back and leading me to a bench on the right side of the line. "Stay here," he says. "I'll be right back."

He disappears, and I place the flowers on the bench beside me, looking down at my socks on the gray floor of the airport. I'm aware of people laughing, Christmas carols in the background, but I just stare at my feet, feeling numb. I sometimes hear women say how sick they are of men. Well, I guess for me that's true. Luke has literally made me sick. Did I even pack my toothbrush? Do I have a mint? I'm not sure what's more disgusting: the taste in my mouth or the disgust in my heart for the entire male population.

I can't remember the last time Jax and I spent any real time alone together. High school, I guess. He was my best friend. He probably knows me better than Luke. In fact, I'm sure he does, but Jax broke my heart long before Luke did. I had a huge crush on Jax. It's hard not to—dark hair, blue eyes, and muscles to write home about, plus he's smart and funny. He's the full package, except that he's an asshole.

Senior year, after months of flirting, I asked him to take me to prom. Yep, *I asked him*, thinking that was very modern and bold of me. He turned me down. Actually, that wasn't the bad part. He told me he wasn't going because he didn't want to ask his mom for the money to rent the tuxedo, tickets, dinner and everything else that goes along with it. I understood. My parents were both teachers, and he was raised by a single mom. We weren't like Maci, Malcolm, and Luke, who all lived in the gated subdivision together where designer labels were par for the course.

Maybe that's why Jax and I bonded so quickly. We got each other. Or I thought we did until he showed up at prom, tuxedo and all, with another girl. It crushed me. He and I haven't been the same since. We maintain a friendship mostly because we have the same circle of friends. If it weren't for that, I don't think I would've spoken to him again after that big of a diss.

What the hell is he doing here now?

Checking my phone, I see Maci's messages about the twins being sick, explaining that she's sending Jax, and how sorry she is. She's got the biggest heart. Of course, her kids come first. I ignore the rest of the messages, all of which are from Luke.

Lowering my suitcase to the floor, I kneel beside it, unzipping the front pocket, hunting for my toiletries, hoping to find my toothbrush and toothpaste. The only things I find are some socks, my flat iron, and a random deck of cards. Good Lord, I was really spaced out when I packed.

Next, I unzip the main compartment, flipping open the lid. Throwing things about, I dig to the bottom. "Um." Jax clears his throat, holding up a pair of black G-string panties that I must've tossed a little too far.

I snatch them from his hand. "I was looking for my toothbrush."

"Those could be dental floss, maybe," he snickers.

I'm really in no mood, and the look I give him tells him so. Unfazed, he holds out a cute little travel pack with a toothbrush and toothpaste inside that I know he must've just purchased from the airport store. I'm officially a bitch.

"I rinsed off your shoes," he says, holding them up. "The laces are still wet, but . . ." he shrugs a little.

I thank him, grateful for his thoughtfulness, but thoughts work both ways, and while he's being sweet now, my mind won't ever forget watching him dancing with that other girl, a huge, cocky grin on his face. The male species just sucks!

∼

IT'S A GOOD forty minutes from the Pensacola airport to the town of Waterscape. So after I got myself together at the airport, I put on my sunglasses and settle in for the drive, resting my head on the window, my subtle hint to Jax that I don't want to talk. My seatmate on the airplane hadn't gotten the hint and blabbed the whole flight. I think he was afraid of flying and talking made him feel better, so I humored him, but I really just wanted peace and quiet.

Lightly, I play with the petals on the flowers Jax brought me. The same ones he sends me on my birthday every year—Irises. Growing up, our moms always had them in our yards, both of them sharing a love of gardening. It's sweet that he always remembers, but I never understood why he sends them. We aren't nearly as close as we used to be.

The ones he sent me this year were still on the coffee table in my apartment when I left. My birthday was a few weeks ago, but for some reason, I was unable to throw them out this year. Maybe it was because I broke things off with Luke on my birthday and wanted something nice to look at. Maybe it was because I didn't know when I'd get flowers from a man again. Who knows? But now I have fresh ones sitting in my lap.

"Have you talked to your mom?" Jax asks. "Does she know you

are coming in?"

I shake my head. My parents were older when they had me, and my dad passed away when I was in college. I didn't know it at the time, but my mom had been diagnosed with Multiple Sclerosis. She lives in an assisted living center now. She's still one of the youngest people there, but they have skilled nurses that can help her when she needs it. It's a nice place, more like a country club, but I hate that I'm so far away. It's another reason why I come back as much as I can.

"I saw her last week," Jax says. "She looked good."

She told me he stopped by. He stops by to visit with her at least once a week. His mom wasn't exactly a typical mom. She partied a lot, dated a lot. She's a sweet lady, and I love her, but she is always searching for love in all the wrong places. Currently, she's searching for it in Alaska. Jax was always close to my parents. My parents helped his mom out with him while she worked, and she returned the favor when they needed help with me. Still, I think Jax thinks of my mom as a surrogate mom.

"I don't want her to worry," I say. "I'm going to make my visit like I'm surprising her."

"Always the trooper," he says, looking over and flashing me a smile.

"I'm fine," I lie. "I was just airsick."

"Okay," he says, letting me get away with my little fib. "Here we are."

I look up as he waves to the security guard at the gate, who recognizes him. Following the rounding road through the same neighborhood where Malcolm and Maci grew up, every house looks like it comes out of a magazine, all dressed up for Christmas. Some in red and white, others green and gold, still others in ice blue, but all of them perfect. I remember thinking when I was younger that this is where the perfect people lived. Didn't take me long to figure out that what my parents had was perfect, and this was all just window dressing.

We park in front of Maci and Malcolm's house. We used to call them M&M's in high school. Between their names and their level of sweetness with each other, it was fitting. Maci works with me and stays at home with her kids, and Malcolm is some sort of computer wizard IT guy. Until very recently, I didn't even realize that IT stands for Information Technology, so you can guess how much I know about his job. All I know is that he gets paid big bucks by big companies to do something on the computer, and that he works from home.

Their house is a two-story colonial decorated with red and green wreaths and plastic candy canes lining the path to their front door. It's just a few streets away from where Maci and Malcolm's parents still live. Built-in babysitters, Maci calls them.

Jax opens his car door, starting to walk around to get mine, as I see Maci step outside the house. Not waiting for Jax, I fling open the car door. I'm anxious to get one of her huge hugs, only she holds her hands up, a medical mask covering her face.

"I may be covered in stomach flu germs," she says.

That doesn't stop me for a moment, and before I know it, we have each other wrapped in a hug, her bright red hair mixing with my brown like we are one person. Jax, on the other hand, keeps his distance, and I'm not sure if it's because of the germs or because he wants to give me some privacy.

"How are the kids?" I ask, pulling back to get a look at her. Her skin is as pale as mine, only she's got freckles that I always thought were adorable, but she hates them. Maybe that's why we were such fast friends. Pigment-challenged people have to stick together.

She shrugs. "They're bad, but now Malcolm has it, too." She flashes a look to Jax, and he steps a little closer. "Skylar, you know you are welcome here anytime, and I want you to stay, but I don't want you to get sick."

I usually stay here when I come into town. My mom isn't allowed overnight guests at the assisted living center. I've got nowhere else to go, but the last thing I need is to get sick. I've already thrown up once today.

"I feel like such a crap friend," she says. "I insisted you come here. I know you need some girl time, and I'm just . . ." she trails off as she flicks the fabric of her stained shirt.

"It's okay. I'm sure I can find a hotel."

Again, her eyes go to Jax. No, don't even think it.

"She can stay with me," he says.

"No," I blurt out. "I'll find a hotel."

"I called around," Maci says. "It's the holidays. Things are booked up or super expensive."

I glance back at Jax then give Maci the evil eye. "There has to be something."

"There's Jax," she whispers. "Just for a few days until everyone is better, then you can come stay here."

~

FROM THE FRONT seat of Jax's car, I watch Maci giving him instructions like she's leaving her kids with a new babysitter, only I know she's talking about me. Maybe I should've stayed in Chicago, it might've been less torturous than having to stay with Jax. I left one man who broke my heart to go stay with the original heartbreaker. Fabulous!

Maci hands Jax a bag, and he peeks inside before glancing over his shoulder at me waiting. He turns and starts walking toward his car. Jax has money now, but you wouldn't know it by his car. Don't get me wrong, it's a nice luxury SUV, which I'm sure carries a hefty price tag, but you'd think a young bachelor with his money would be driving around in something to attract women, not something that you might find in a school carpool lane. Granted, it might be the most expensive thing in the carpool lane, but still.

Hopping in the car, he hands me the bag. "Maci says this is the essential breakup kit."

I peek inside finding wine, whiskey, ice cream, nail polish, and drug store facial masks. God, I love her.

"There it is," Jax says, motioning to my face. "The dimple."

I try not to, but feel my smile grow. It's short-lived when I hear my cell phone ringing out from my purse. Luke again. Forcefully, I hit the decline button and snap, "Isn't there some rule about how many times you should call your ex?"

"Depends," he says.

"On what?" I ask.

"If you truly believe she's the one."

His blue eyes catch mine. "Luke doesn't think I'm the love of his life. Trust me."

"Luke has been in love with you since we were twelve," he says, putting the car in drive.

"I don't want to talk about him," I say. The phone rings again. "I just want him to stop calling me."

"Give me your phone," he says, shifting the car back to park. I just stare at him. He holds his hand out. The next ring seals the deal, and I hand it to him. He punches a few buttons then hands it back to me. "He's blocked."

"You blocked his number?" I cry out.

"You don't want to hear from him, right?" he asks. Suddenly, I feel confused. "Or maybe you like knowing he's calling? That he's missing you."

"No," I say, needing his barrage of calls to stop. "I'm through with him."

"You're sure?" he asks.

I'm very sure and feel myself smile again. "I can't believe you blocked your friend."

"Guess this means I'm on your side," he says with a chuckle, starting to drive.

"No, Jax," I cry and reach out to touch his arm. As soon as my fingers feel the hard muscles, I snap back. "I don't want this to affect your friendship with him. I told Maci and Malcolm the same thing. I'm not sure how this will all work out, but I don't want you guys to have to take sides. No team Luke, team Skylar."

His head shakes. "How about you don't worry about everyone else and focus on yourself for a few days?"

"I'm really . . ."

"Yeah, I know you're fine," he teases me. "Christmas is a less than a week away. Give this gift to yourself. We'll make it Skylar's Christmas week."

"That's not necessary," I say. "You don't need to babysit me. I know you're probably working on some deadline."

He shrugs. "I've got a seminar tomorrow night, but that's it until after the New Year. My mission this week is you."

"Jax," I whisper, feeling my throat tightening up.

"I know," he says, his hand landing on mine. "You're fine."

CHAPTER THREE

JAX

I'VE GOT NO idea what went down between Skylar and Luke, and I'm not going to ask. Even though Skylar and I haven't been as close as we once were, I know her. She'll only tell me when she's ready.

I never thought Skylar and I would sleep under the same roof again. When we were kids, we had "sleepovers" all the time. Then as teenagers, I used to climb out my window, traverse the roof's edge, and sneak into her bedroom. More often than not, we fell asleep with me on her floor. Nothing ever happened between us. Nothing except talking for hours, laughing together, sharing everything with each other.

It's funny how sometimes nothing means everything.

Those nights in her room were the best part of my day—better than football practice, hanging with the guys, making out with other girls. Doing "nothing" with Skylar was what I lived for back then. I've got a chance to get a little of that back, and I'm not about to blow it.

She rolls the car window down as soon as we get close to the beach. I look over at her, the wind whipping her hair around like a leaf caught in a breeze. Her eyes are closed, and her full pink lips have the slightest hint of a smile, like she knows a secret.

I hit the button in my car that activates my garage door, and that brings Skylar back to the present. As I pull inside, she leans out, trying to catch a glimpse of the outside of the house. "I always did love this house," she says.

I just smile, knowing it was her favorite. I know all her favorites—movies, songs, cereal, color, flower. My house isn't the biggest on the beach. It isn't the newest, but all those other houses weren't loved by Skylar, so when this one came on the market, I didn't think twice about buying it. No one knows that, not even Skylar.

"You just moved in, right?"

"About a month ago. It's not totally furnished yet," I say, realizing that I don't have an extra bed for her, and I doubt she's going to want to share. Hopping out of the car, Skylar doesn't wait for me to get her door. I really wish she would. I'm going to have to be quicker.

Instead, I grab her suitcase, open the door to the house, and lead her inside. From the garage, you enter a mudroom that flows into the kitchen. As soon as you step foot in the kitchen, the view of the water hits you. The kitchen and den are one big space. The walls are white, the floors a gray hardwood, and the stairs leading to the second floor have a clear wall so everything looks open and vast like the view.

"It's beautiful, Jax," she says. "Really beautiful."

It is, but I can't rip my eyes away from her. The water will always be there, but Skylar won't be. I remind myself that she's Luke's Skylar, not mine. Even if they're broken up, that's the bro code. That's what we live by. That's what kept us friends all these years. We don't go after each other's women—ever. I can't do that to Luke. He's one of my closest friends. Besides, Skylar's recovering from a breakup. I won't be her rebound.

Not that she'd give me a shot, anyway. I hurt her years ago, and she hasn't forgotten that. Hurt sticks with a person longer than love does. Skylar and I were never more than friends, but we meant a lot to one another. That all disappeared when I hurt her. One hurt wiped out years of love. How much love will it take to wipe out the hurt?

I'm the gentleman behind the handbook, but I don't have a damn clue.

"Do you think I can just go to sleep?" she asks, her voice soft. She must see the confused look on my face. It's barely seven o'clock. "I didn't get much sleep last night."

"You don't want to eat anything?" I ask. "I have strict orders from Maci to not let you be alone too much and to make you eat."

"Sleep," she says. "Please."

I cave. I'm a pushover when it comes to her. God help me if she ever figures that out. Taking her bag, I motion toward the stairs. Looking around, she slowly walks up. I'm not going to look at her perfect ass. I'm not. I'm keeping my eyes on the floor.

"Double doors on the right," I say.

She nods a little. I step in front of her so I can get the door. Waiting for her to enter first, she just peeks inside. The view is the same as downstairs. It might even be better from up here. The bed centers the room, and unlike the color scheme downstairs, the wood tones of the furniture are dark, the bedding a gray-blue color.

"This is *your* room," she says, not stepping inside.

I'm not sure how she can tell that, unless she's just guessing based on the size. I don't have any personal photos around, no clothes on the floor to tip her off. I go inside, laying her suitcase down on the bed. "Remember I told you the house wasn't furnished yet? This is the only bedroom."

"I'm not taking your bed," she says.

"Yeah, you are," I say, surprised at the stern tone in my voice.

"I can just sleep on the sofa," she says. "I'll feel guilty if I kick you out of your own bed."

"I'll take the sofa," I say, grinning at her. "It's a step up from your bedroom floor." Her blue eyes soften. She remembers those nights, too, and she remembers them fondly. If I want to mend things with her, I need to keep reminding her of what we shared. "And I won't have to listen to you snore."

She breaks into a full-on laugh. The first one I've seen from her. There is something special about seeing a woman you care about happy. It's the most addictive experience.

Gentleman's Rule: *If hearing her laugh doesn't make your top ten reasons for living, then you probably shouldn't be with her.*

She yawns through her laugh, and I ask, "You need anything

else?"

She shakes her head, but I'm not ready to leave her. I point out the master bathroom, telling her where the towels are, and then I just stand there like a moron. I'm around beautiful, sexy women all the time, but none of them make me speechless, render me an idiot. One afternoon with Skylar, and I'm suddenly a mute.

"Thank you," she says.

"Any time," I say, hating that she thanked me. I mean, it's sweet she did, and Skylar's always a grateful person, but I hate the formality of her gratitude. It's almost like she's dismissing me. She used to thank me with a hug or a kiss on the cheek. This time I half-expected a handshake, and just when I thought I was getting somewhere.

∽

IT'S BEEN NEARLY fifteen hours since I've seen Skylar, and other than the shower turning on last night, I haven't heard any noise coming from upstairs. Maybe the house is just so soundproof that I can't hear her. Should I check on her? Maci's already called three times. If I don't put Skylar on the phone next time she calls, she's liable to come over here and strangle me.

I've got a seminar to give tonight about an hour away in Panama City. Much like a music concert, the outline of the dialogue stays the same, so I don't really have to do much to prepare other than brush up on my notes, which I did last night. Things can always go off the rails at these things, especially during the question and answer portion, but I'm very quick on my feet. I worked out this morning, ate breakfast. I even put away my pillow and blanket from my night on the sofa. Basically, I'm just waiting for her. It's as if the day won't really start until I see Skylar.

Mostly, I've been thinking about what to do while she's here for the holidays. Christmas in a beach town is a little different than in the rest of the country. Add in that the beach is in the South, and basically any traditional thoughts of snow and hot chocolate go out the window. Still, Waterscape has its own traditions, starting with the bonfire on the beach tonight. Hopefully, I make it back in time so Skylar doesn't have to watch it solo.

My cell phone dings with a text.

Hope I'm not waking you. I couldn't sleep, so I took a cab to come see my mom. Thanks for the bed last night. C U later, Skylar.

What the hell? She's not even here! I've been up since at least seven, so she must've snuck out with the roosters. I was hoping to spend some time with her today, but I can't begrudge her seeing her mom.

There was a little connection with us last night. I know she felt that. Perhaps she didn't like remembering how she used to feel about me. We both know she felt more than friendship. I imagine those feelings would be uncomfortable right now, since she's staying at my house and coming off a breakup. But those feelings are what I'm counting on. I want her to remember—to remember how she feels about me.

∽

I'M BACKSTAGE WAITING. I can hear the bustle of the crowd taking their seats and can't believe all these people are here just a few days before Christmas. At least this one is close to home, only an hour drive. This is my last gig for a while, then I can focus on Christmas and Skylar.

I didn't hear from Skylar all day. I checked to see if she needed a ride home, but other than her *Thank you, I'm good* text, I didn't hear a word.

My cell phone rings, and I reach for it, needing to switch it off anyway, and see Skylar's calling. I've only got a few minutes until I need to start, but I'll keep a crowd of five hundred paying customers waiting for Skylar any day.

"What do you have to do to get a ticket to this thing?" she says with a sassy little laugh.

"You're here?" I ask in disbelief.

"Yeah, I took a cab. I wanted to see you in action, but apparently the line of bullshit you sell is sold out."

This is why us men need handbooks and rules for relationships. The same woman who disappeared out of my house this morning just took a cab an hour to come see me! Females are confusing. Laughing, I say, "Think I can work something out. Give me two minutes."

Quickly, I find the organizer and explain that I need an extra seat. Within a couple minutes, I peek through the curtain, seeing Skylar being led to a seat off to the side near the back of the room. I hear my introduction being made and know this is my chance to say some things to her. Things I need to say. Things that aren't in my usual presentation, but fuck it!

"Please help me give a warm welcome to the Gentleman himself, Jax Teigan."

I step out onto the stage to applause. It's a smaller venue tonight—a college auditorium. The lights aren't blinding. I can see every face in the crowd, but it's only Skylar's I care about. Like most nights, the audience is full of women. Not bragging or anything, but I don't often leave these things without at least a few dozen phone numbers. I'm convinced at least half these women are here looking to marry me.

"I'm going to do something a little different tonight," I say, taking off my suit jacket.

Some of the women start to scream like I'm going to strip, and I see Skylar roll her eyes. "How many of you can tell me the first rule of being a gentleman?"

Collectively, they all scream out, "Smack her ass every day."

I laugh out. That was the first rule of the first book I ever wrote, and probably one of the most popular rules.

"That's right. But you all know what that rule really means?"

The crowd quiets down. "It means as men, we have to let our wives, our girlfriends, know every day how we feel about them.

However we need to do that. Whether it's to smack their ass, tell them we love them, or do the fucking dishes."

The crowd goes into a roar.

Gentleman's Rule—*Nothing sexier than a man who helps with housework. Pussy guaranteed!*

"Show of hands. How many of you are currently not in a relationship?" I ask, watching Skylar.

She looks around at the crowd then slowly lifts her hand in the air with about fifty percent of the room.

"I'm going to tell you something. Something that's going to change your life. Everyone ready?"

Another deafening cheer.

I wait a moment before I take a step forward on the stage, my eyes zeroing in on Skylar. "It's not about you." The crowd goes stone cold quiet. "That's right. It's not about you."

They all start to look around at each other.

"You haven't found love," I say. "And that's not about you."

Skylar's hand goes to her mouth.

"A man's refusal to love you back or make a commitment has nothing to do with you. It's his shit, not yours."

I watch the crowd think for a second then start nodding their heads. If there's one thing I've learned about women since starting this career, it's that as a species, they are hard on themselves. Some asshole hits them, it's their fault. Their kid makes a bad grade, it's their fault. The ozone is depleting, it's their hairspray! Seriously, women can blame themselves for anything and everything. So naturally, if a guy doesn't return their feelings, they think it has something to do with them without even considering that it's the guy's fault! Sure, some women don't let it affect them, but those women don't come see me speak. I preach to the choir before me.

"In fact, I've got a new gentleman rule for you tonight. You guys are the first ones to hear it. Ready?"

The crowd goes crazy.

Gentleman's Rule—*If you don't love her, someone else will.*

Even though Skylar's seated in the back of the room, I still see her wipe her eyes. She's not the only one in the room. It breaks my heart a little. Does she worry that no one will ever love her? If she only knew.

"And you better be prepared to watch it. Trust me on this one. It's the worst feeling in the world to watch someone you love with someone else, knowing no one could love her better than you."

∼

"YOU'RE LIKE A rock star or something," Skylar says, smiling over at me as we walk inside my house. She's talked non-stop since we left my seminar, the entire drive back together. It's amazing to see her happy and not thinking about Luke. We picked up too many pizzas, too much beer, and are just getting home in time to watch the bonfire on the beach.

"Hardly," I say.

"That one woman had you sign her boob!" she says, putting the pizzas down on the kitchen island.

"I've signed worse," I say, raising an eyebrow.

"Seriously? What's she going to do, never wash her boobs again? She obviously just wanted you to see her boob job."

"It was a nice boob job, as far as they go," I tease her.

"Why do guys like fake boobs?" she asks, looking down at the chest God gave her.

She's on the smaller side of the tit alphabet. I'm guessing a full B maybe, but they fit her, very nicely. Not that I'm looking.

"We like tits. We don't really care if they're natural, silicone, or saline."

"Dear God," she says, slipping her shoes off.

That simple act makes my heart thunder, liking that she's comfortable here in my house with me. I like it a little too much.

"You don't have a Christmas tree," she says.

"It's just me," I say, grabbing the pizzas and beer. "I don't usually decorate." I head toward the sliding glass door. She hurries to open the door for me, and we step onto the patio, the pool glistening in the moonlight.

"I'm glad we didn't miss it," she says, looking around for somewhere to sit.

I haven't gotten around to patio furniture yet, so I nod my head for her to sit on the one lounge chair. She lowers it so it's completely flat then sits down all the way at one end, taking the pizza from me and putting it in the middle.

Placing the beer on the ground, I sit opposite her and lift the lid. It was our thing when we were younger that I always let her pick the first piece. Somehow it turned into her trying to pick the piece I have my eye on. It's like searching for the best french fry, some just look better than others. I eye a piece close to me. I don't actually want that piece. It's got one of those giant bubbles on it, so there are no toppings in that section. That's the worst slice, but I want her to think that's the slice I want.

She's too smart for me and takes the cheesiest piece in the box. "You're eating that bubble piece," I say, taking the next best slice.

She laughs, and it's like no time has passed at all. We might as well be right back in her teenage bedroom. "You did an amazing job tonight," she says. "I don't think I realized how huge you've become until sitting in a room with all those women loving on you."

I just shrug. It's a job. The fact is, I don't know more than anyone else about love. I've just packaged it better.

People come and go in our lives. There might be someone you think you can't live without and then one day you realize you haven't thought about them in forever. Happens all the time with friends, lovers, even family. Then there are the people that stick. No matter what you do, how hard you work, how you distract yourself, who you screw, you can't shake them.

Skylar is the one woman that has stuck to me. No matter what I do, I haven't ever been able to exorcise the pull I feel to her. It was easier to deny it when she was with Luke, telling myself she was happy with him, but now I find her single, in my house, and the pull to her I've tried so hard to suppress is raging—in my cock, in my head, but no place is stronger than my heart.

"Seriously, you know what you said tonight about it not being about me?" she asks.

This is good. She realized I was talking to her. Does she realize everything I said was directed to her?

"Yeah."

"Luke didn't want to marry me," she says, glancing away. "That's why I broke up with him."

"Are you sure he . . ."

"Ten years," she says, shaking her head. "I promised myself last Christmas that I wouldn't spend another Christmas with him unless we were engaged."

"Did he know that?" I ask.

"No," she says. "I made a promise to myself that I wouldn't give him an ultimatum. I wanted him to *want* to marry me, not ask me because I made him."

"Makes sense."

"All our friends are getting married. Do you know we went to ten weddings last year? Ten! Now the baby showers are starting. Nothing from Luke. He never even asked me to move in or anything. At some point, a girl has to cut her losses."

"So you just left?"

She shakes her head. "On my birthday a few weeks ago, I was convinced he was going to ask me. He told me he had something big to tell me. I thought for sure it was a proposal. Turns out, he forgot my birthday altogether. The big announcement was that he got a job offer in Paris. He wanted me to move there with him. Go there for Christmas to check it out."

"What did you say?"

"I laughed. I didn't mean to. I think I was just in shock," she says. "He got pretty pissed off after that."

I know there's more she's not telling me. That was weeks ago. If she was torn up, she would've come home before now.

"All this time, I'm thinking *what's wrong with me that he won't propose?* Tonight, what you said, it just made me feel better."

"Luke is an idiot," I say. "He should've married you years ago."

"You're one to talk," she says. "You wouldn't even take me to prom."

She says it playfully, but I can hear the pain. "That was different."

"Doesn't matter now," she says.

"You want the truth?" I ask, and she nods. "I couldn't go with you because Luke liked you. He was my best friend. I couldn't do that to him. We had a rule about that."

There was no way I could go with her. Luke had been trying to get up the courage to ask her for weeks. Besides, I thought she was only asking me as a friend. I didn't realize until later that she felt the same way about me that I felt about her. I didn't know that until I saw the look on her face when I walked in with another girl. It was already too late—too late to explain that I didn't want to be there with anyone but her, too late to explain that my mom forced me to go, not wanting me to miss a "rite of passage," too late to tell her that my mom had been saving up so that I could have a good time. It was too late for all that. The damage was done, the hurt in her eyes told me that. Even if I could explain back then, there was Luke.

"That's really the reason?" she asks, and I nod. "So if he hadn't liked me, then you would've said yes?"

"No," I say, catching her eyes. "I would've asked you first."

I want nothing more than to lean in and kiss her. All the reasons why I can't are still there, but in the moment, I don't care. It's dangerous, and most importantly, there is no way Skylar is ready for me to kiss her.

"Look," she says, pointing down the beach at the bonfire starting. I think there's something like thirty miles of beach that light fires. It's cool to sit back and watch the flames all begin like a glorious wave in a football stadium. When the Waterscape fire is lit, you can hear the screams on my patio.

I look back over at Skylar, finding her staring at me, seeing something in her eyes that I haven't seen in a long time. Forgiveness.

That's what I wanted. The problem is, I know it won't be enough. I want her.

Rules or no rules. Bro code or not, I know all I want for Christmas this year and every year is Skylar.

CHAPTER FOUR

SKYLAR

A LOUD THUD jolts me awake. Sitting up in bed, I hear it again. What could Jax be doing at this hour? How is he not tired? He worked last night, then we stayed up watching the bonfire.

For the most part, I've thought the "Gentleman's Rules" are complete bullshit until last night. Jax may be the poster boy for bachelors, but there is truth behind some of what he says. Judging by what he told me about prom and Luke, clearly, he lives the rules. I always assumed he just didn't want to take me, not that he didn't want to step on Luke's toes. I can't really be mad at Jax for that, at least not anymore.

I was so proud watching him last night. The little boy I used to play with every day has turned into a self-help heartthrob. I've seen an online video here or there of him, but I've never heard him speak live. He's charming by nature. Good looking as the day is long. Dress him up in a suit, and damn, there wasn't a woman in the room that wasn't swooning. Women love a man in a suit. There's even a term for it—suit porn.

The floor vibrates with another bang from downstairs. Yawning, I get out of bed and open the bedroom door, finding Jax coming up the stairs. He flashes me a cocky grin, a look in his eyes like he's up to something.

"Skylar's Christmas week has officially begun!" he says, taking my hand and pulling me down the stairs, the tallest, fattest Christmas tree I've ever seen in the middle of his den.

"You said I needed a tree."

"I didn't say a Giant Sequoia!" I giggle.

His head tilts, looking at it. "Yeah, it is a little big."

"Compensating for something," I tease him.

"My wood is . . ."

"Oh my God," I say, slapping him playfully.

"Just call me Sequoia!" he boasts.

"You wish." He just laughs at me, pulling me around the tree, and after a moment, I realize he hasn't let go of my hand. Does he realize that?

"I got it in here and realized that I don't have a single decoration."

Releasing his hand, I head toward the stairs and say, "No problem. I have my parents' ornaments stored in Maci and Malcolm's garage. I'll call them."

∞

"THE RED PLASTIC containers," I say, pointing them out to Jax.

Maci's garage looks like it was put together by a professional organizer, so it's not hard to find what we need. Jax starts moving the containers down from the shelf. I can see the muscles of his back and shoulders flex as he moves, and know I shouldn't be noticing that. He's my friend. He's my ex's friend. He's also the sexiest man I've ever seen in person. You always see pictures online of hot guys at the beach, male models in magazines, movie stars, but I've never actually seen a guy who looks like that in person, except for Jax. He makes all those other guys look like boys. I shake my head at myself. I'm here to mend my broken heart, not ogle the opposite sex.

"You look so much better," Maci says to me.

"I'm feeling better," I say. "How's everyone feeling here?"

"Better," Maci says. "I think you're safe to come stay here. I've got your room all ready."

A strange sensation flutters through my body. I always stay at Maci's. It's like a second home, but the thought of leaving Jax's house throws me off. He just got the tree for me. We're decorating today. A little voice inside my head whispers, *you know it's more than that.*

"Why would she do that?" Jax says, giving me a little wink. "Crying, screaming kids or an ocean view?"

"You have a point," Maci says. "Can I come stay at your house, too?"

Laughing, I say, "I'm good at Jax's house, but I miss you."

"Let's go out tonight," she says. "Malcolm, me, you two. I'll get my mom to watch the kids. It's Christmas Karaoke tonight at Water's Edge!"

I slap my forehead with the palm of my hand. "Don't you remember what happened two years ago? I'm not sure they'll let us back in!"

"My voice isn't that bad!" she laughs.

"Yes, it is," Jax chimes in, pulling down another box. "That poor man's eardrum burst."

"That had nothing to do with my singing!" Maci laughs out. "Come on. It will be fun!"

"I'm going to regret this."

"Regret is good," Maci says, elbowing me. "You don't have enough regrets."

"This coming from the gal who's dated the same boy since she was twelve."

Rolling her eyes, she says, "And don't forget that Santa's Jingle Run is tomorrow morning."

The Jingle Run is a Waterscape tradition. The whole town comes out to raise money to purchase gifts for kids who are in the hospital at Christmas. Everyone dresses crazy, Santa is there, and it's a lot of fun. "You did not register me for that!"

"Yeah," she says. "We are all running. Malcolm and I are pushing the kids in the stroller."

"I suppose you have my costume, too?" I ask but already know the answer.

Maci and I used to do the Jingle Run every year, and every year she'd make me wear some outrageous costume. We've run it in reindeer costumes, glittery pink Santa hats, sneakers that look like elf shoes. We even ran it once with mistletoe hanging from the top of our heads.

"Red bikini!" she says, raising an eyebrow at me. We always despised the girls that showed off and ran the race in barely-there swimsuits. It's a charity run, not a runway.

"I will if you will," I dare her, thinking there is no way in heck she's going to show up in a red bikini.

Maci shimmies her boobs at me. "These things are way too big to be bouncing around the streets of Waterscape. I'm liable to kill someone."

~

STANDING BACK, I look up at my parents' Christmas decorations hanging on Jax's tree. My parents bought me a new ornament every year during the holidays in addition to the ones that they bought whenever we took a trip, so I have quite a collection. Each ornament is like a little walk down memory lane. I never took them to Chicago when I moved, it just didn't seem like their home.

This is their home. Waterscape.

It's good to see them hanging up again. It should feel strange seeing them up on Jax's tree, but it doesn't. He's part of a lot of these memories, too. There's the ornament my parents bought me when my family, Jax, and his mom traveled to the Atlanta zoo together when we were only in grade school. There's the ornament he helped me make for my parents one Christmas out of seashells. Each ornament is a trip back into our childhood.

This is what a Christmas tree should look like. I always admire the trees in the stores that look so perfect. I've been in houses where the trees look much the same, and they are lovely, but this is what Christmas is about—family and home.

Jax and I have spent most of the day decorating the tree together.

I haven't decorated a tree with someone since I lived at home with my parents. Luke and I didn't live together, so I always just did my own tree. He never bothered to put one up, claiming he was too busy. He'd think I was crazy if I told him I spent a whole day doing this, but you know what, I wouldn't change this day for the world. Jax and I ordered Chinese takeout, played Christmas music, spent at least an hour trying to figure out which bulb was loose on a strand of lights, then laughed at ourselves for taking so long. It was the most fun I've had in a long time.

Luke's idea of fun always involved big things, like trips, concerts, sporting events. Those are great, but simple fun is more my speed—no packing, no high heels, no fussy clothes. I was in sweats and a t-shirt all day. It was fabulous.

I only hope karaoke will be as much fun. Usually karaoke night involves having to drag Maci off the stage. Let's just say, she enjoys the limelight a little too much.

"You look great!" Jax tells me, grabbing his keys off the kitchen counter.

I just exchanged my sweats and t-shirt for jeans and an oversized sweater. I'm hardly a fashionista. It's not a smack on my ass, but is he trying to play by his rules with me? I really don't care if he is. A compliment is a compliment. I'll take it.

I thank him, not paying him the same compliment—though he looks drop dead hot. He always does, but it's not my place to say. "Promise me you won't let Maci drag me up on stage with her?"

"I promise," Jax says, placing his hand at the small of my back, leading me outside.

The bar is only about a half mile down the beach from Jax's house, so we decide to walk along the sand. Flip-flops in hand, I roll up my jeans in case a wave catches me, and we head toward the red lights of the bar. I look up at the moon, the stars, the Waterscape sky looking so different from the Chicago sky.

I love the ocean, the beach, but not at night. Once the sun sets, it goes from peaceful and serene to a black abyss. I like the water during the day when you can see to the bottom. I like seeing what's coming. In the dark, you've got no idea. Danger could be right in front of you, and you wouldn't see it.

"Thinking about moving back here?" Jax asks.

"How'd you know?"

He shrugs. "Your business is here. Your mom. Your friends. It's not hard to figure it out."

"I don't have to decide anything right now."

"Yeah, you do," he says, taking me by the waist and twirling me. "You have to decide what song to sing."

"Know that already. No one beats T. Swift for a breakup song: 'We Are Never Ever Getting Back Together'."

"Think it's supposed to be a Christmas song," he teases, but then he stops, his eyes looking toward the bar. "Do you hear that?"

"No," I say.

He takes my hand, hurrying toward the bar. It's the second time today he's taken me by the hand. Did he used to do that when we were kids?

The bar is on the beach so the windows all open to maximize the view and the breeze, but tonight the windows are allowing noise pollution, too. From the looks of the birds flying away, Maci's on the stage. As soon as we reach the door, Jax releases my hand, opening the door for me. The place is filled with people. Nothing like celebrating the Christmas spirit with a few spirits of the liquid variety.

Malcolm waves to us from a booth, shaking his head at his wife who is already on the stage belting out "The Twelve Days of Christmas." Leave it to Maci to pick the longest song she can find to stretch her time in the spotlight.

The bar is packed tonight. Everyone is laughing and singing along. Red Christmas lights cascade across the ceiling. Tinsel is tossed on anything and everything. The waitresses are all wearing sexy Santa skirts with knee high black boots, and best of all, I'm here with my best friends.

Malcolm gets to his feet, wrapping me in a hug. He's clean-shaven, unlike the slight stubble Jax always sports. He's tall like Jax, but his ginger hair matches his wife's perfectly. He's the quietest of our group. When you are around Malcolm, you get the feeling he's watching everything and taking it all in.

"I have no control," he says, pointing to his wife, who is currently doing a very provocative dance to the line about the maids milking.

"I'd hate to see her performance to 'The Little Drummer Boy'!" I say.

"Don't give her any ideas," Malcolm says as we all take our seats. From the looks of things, it's going to be a long night.

"How much has she had to drink?" Jax asks, unable to take his eyes off the train wreck that is Maci's performance.

"Nothing," Malcolm says with a laugh. "You know Maci, she's on a natural high."

Jax raises his hand up, motioning to the waitress. "Another?" he asks Malcolm, who nods. He orders beers for himself and Malcolm then looks at me.

I look around at what other people are drinking. "I want that pink one," I say, pointing to another waitress walking by with a tray of drinks.

"That's our Christmas special, Jingle Juice," the waitress says.

"Perfect," I say. She flashes a smile to Jax then walks to the bar to get our drinks. "You know her?"

He shakes his head. "Did you really just order a drink based solely on color?"

"Of course," I say. "Oh crap, I should've ordered one for Maci."

"Ordered me what?" she asks, scooting in beside Malcolm.

I should've realized she was finished. I can hear myself think now. "Jingle Juice."

Maci looks at Malcolm, who smiles then gives her a little shrug and head tilt, as if to say it's her call. "So I'm pregnant again," Maci says like it's the most common thing in the world to say.

I'm totally the friend to tell things to if you want a big, over the top reaction, and tonight is no exception. My scream rivals the ocean waves. I'm up out of my seat, hugging them both, a zillion questions coming out of my mouth.

"How far along? When are you due? Why didn't you tell me? Is it a secret?"

Maci holds her hands up, giving Jax an opportunity to congratulate them both, then she fills me in on the details. She's due in the early summer. It's not a secret, and she wanted to tell me in person. The waitress returns with our drinks, and we have a toast to celebrate the news.

Maci looks at Malcolm again, and he gives her an encouraging nod. It's sweet to watch them together, the unspoken support. "So we're going to have to talk about the business," she says. "It's hard enough with the twins, and now I'm going to have a newborn."

On top of that, I know that Maci doesn't need to work. Malcolm makes good money. I'm not sure what I'd do without her, though. I lean back in the booth, right into Jax's arm, which is resting on the back. His hand wraps around my shoulder, pulling me a little closer, giving me his support, knowing the last thing I need right now is work drama. It's the one thing that's steady.

I glance over at him, searching for my own rock, my own person to lean on. He used to be that person for me, and I still see it in his eyes now. I down my drink. "We'll do what we have to do." I reach across and take Maci's hand. "It will be fine."

"It's just I know we can't really afford to hire . . ." Maci starts before a few tears fall from her eyes.

"You're having a baby," I say, patting her hand. "This is a happy moment."

"But . . ."

"With everything going on, I've been thinking about moving back down here, so maybe this is a sign that it's time."

"Really?" Maci says, her eyes flying to Malcolm again, but she doesn't sound as happy as I thought she would.

Malcolm leans forward a little. "So it's really over with Luke?"

I feel Jax's body tense next to mine. "We broke up."

"I know," Malcolm says. "It's just you've been together so long. Maci and I thought you might work it out."

My head starts to spin a little. It's weird knowing that Luke and I have been the subject of conversations.

"He's torn up," Malcolm says.

Maci elbows him in the side to shut up, but it's too late. "You talked to him?" I ask.

"Earlier," Malcolm says. "He thought for sure you were staying with us."

"You didn't tell him where I am, did you?"

Maci gives her husband a disapproving look. Obviously, Malcolm told him, and Maci's pissed about it. That makes me feel horrible. "I'm sorry you guys are caught in the middle."

"We just thought you two would get back together," Malcolm says.

"Well, I thought that *until* you told me what he did," Maci says.

Jax and Malcolm exchange a glance, both of them in the dark.

"I need another drink," I say, flagging down the waitress.

No one else at my table orders anything. Guess I'm the only lush, but after the week I've had, who cares?

"You know, if I'm honest, Luke and I have been growing apart for a while. I just couldn't let go. It seems stupid, but I had so much time invested in that relationship. It was hard to walk away from that."

"Let's change the subject," Maci says, saving my ass, but putting her husband's in the hot seat. "Malcolm promised to sing tonight!"

CHAPTER FIVE

JAX

"I WANNA GO swimming," Skylar giggles, running down the beach toward my pool.

She had too much Jingle Juice. I catch her by the waist, and she wraps her arms around my neck. There are definite rules about drunk girls. Ones you cannot break, no matter what. So no matter how much I want to kiss her, I won't. I only had one beer for this very reason. I saw the way she downed her first drink, so I didn't drink anything else, knowing I'd need to take care of her. That's far more important than any buzz could ever be. She leans in closer, and I can smell the faint scent of her shampoo.

If I'm not sure she'd kiss me when she's sober, then I can't kiss her now. It's that simple. Still, she's completely adorable. "Think you need to get some sleep," I say, helping her inside and up the stairs to my bedroom.

She pouts her lip at me. "I'm not tired."

"We have the Christmas run tomorrow," I say.

"That girl at the bar tonight liked you," she says, roaming my bedroom aimlessly.

"Which girl?"

"The waitress."

"Not my type," I say, encouraging her to get into bed.

"Oh," she says, hopping up and down a little. "Maci's pregnant!"

I can't help but laugh. "I know."

"I want to have babies," she says, falling on her back into my bed.

Looking down at her, her hair all spread out, a goofy smile on her face, I definitely wouldn't mind some baby-making practice with her.

"Come lay with me," she says, looking up at me. "Like when we were kids. Remember we used to just talk and talk?"

"I remember," I say.

"I miss that," she says, her voice sounding a little sleepy.

Fuck, I miss it, too. I miss it so much.

When Skylar was in Chicago with Luke, it was easier to ignore my feelings for her. Being with her wasn't a possibility, so it was something I just pushed out of my head, forced out of my heart. But when she walked off that airplane, what we could be wasn't just a possibility anymore, it was a reality I want to make happen.

Suddenly, she sits straight up. "Let's stay up all night like we used to. It'll be fun!"

She's impossible to resist. We did this many nights growing up, and I never crossed the line with her. I can do that again. What's one more night?

"Scoot over," I say, and she claps her hands a little before laying down, rolling to her side to face me.

I do the same thing, and she smiles. "We have ten years of secrets to catch up on," she says. "Tell me yours."

"I think I went first last time," I say.

She totally buys that and starts talking. I listen to her tell me about how she secretly hated the earrings Luke bought her last Christmas, who she voted for in the last election, about how one time she put soda in her cup at a fast food restaurant when she only ordered water. She was feeling particularly guilty over that one.

She reaches up and plays with my hair a little, saying, "I have a secret I've kept from you, too."

A dirty one, I hope!

"Christmas twenty years ago." She stops, looking up at the ceiling, the simple math confusing her tipsy mind. "No, nineteen years. Maybe it was twenty-one."

"It doesn't matter," I say, grinning. "Christmas when we were around seven or eight."

"Yeah." She cuddles closer, resting her head against my chest. The temptation just went up tenfold. "We both wanted new bikes, so we could ride to Malcolm and Maci's neighborhood."

"You wanted a pink one," I say.

"You wanted neon green," she says.

"That was the year I stopped believing in Santa Claus," I say. "He didn't bring either one of us a new bike."

"I got a bike that year," she whispers. I look down at her, pushing some of the hair out of her face. "I was so excited to tell you, but then you didn't get one, so I lied to you."

"I never saw a bike."

"I told my parents that I didn't understand why Santa would bring me a bike and not you. I was so upset. I told them you were good all year, better than me."

A few tears roll down her face, and I wipe them away. "Skylar?"

"Mom and Dad broke the news to me about Santa Claus that day," she says. "They told me your mom just couldn't afford to get you a new one that year."

My mom worked hard. I never went without anything I needed. My father died while serving our country. They were young, so he didn't leave her with much, and I was just a baby. She talks about him like he was perfect. She's spent the rest of her life trying to recapture what she had with him. I know it must've hurt her not to be able to get me that bike. She worked as a waitress most of my childhood. Tips were good in the peak summer season, but the winters could be rough.

"I asked my parents to take my bike back," she says softly.

A pain hits my chest. I know how much she wanted that bike. I wanted one just as much. She was just a little kid. That's empathy way beyond her years. Sparing my feelings was more important to her than her own wishes. She loved me that much.

"I didn't want the bike if you couldn't have one, too," she says, yawning a little. "I wanted us to be together."

Why did I ever let Luke ask her out? I'm a fucking idiot. Why did I let him stake some sort of claim to her? We were kids, for fuck's sake. Yes, he's my friend, but she's my . . . She could be my . . .

I look down at her full, pink lips. Leaning in closer, I whisper her name. Her response is a soft, little snore, and I cover my mouth to keep from laughing. Snoring should not make me happy. I shouldn't find it sweet, but with her it is. She is the forbidden fruit. The one woman in the whole garden who I'm not allowed to touch. Sure, she's not with Luke anymore, but no friendship can survive when you date your friend's ex.

Skylar or Luke?

It's an easy choice now, but as a teenager, it wasn't. Luke was my good friend. We played football together, hung out all the time. The five of us were inseparable. But Luke and his family were more than that. I'm not supposed to know. In fact, I don't even know if Luke knows, but his parents paid for my high school tuition each year. There was no way my mom could afford the private school. Skylar would've been in the same boat except both her parents taught at the school, so they got a huge discount. Everyone, including my mom, thought I was on scholarship.

I guess I was. The Luke family scholarship.

It's not a real thing, and I'm not supposed to know, but I overheard his mom and dad talking one day when we were all hanging out at his house. They covered my tuition all through high school simply because I was their son's friend, they knew my mom struggled, they liked me, and they were exceptionally good people, just like their son. No way was I going to betray that and date the girl Luke liked.

Back then, I had no idea the magnitude of what I felt for Skylar. I was a kid. I didn't realize the girl I liked would be the woman I'd love forever.

FOR THE FIRST time, what felt right at night feels even better in the morning. I woke up with Skylar wrapped in my arms. She fell asleep snuggled into my side, and I didn't have the willpower to get up.

I'm awake, but I don't make any attempt to get out of bed, the feel of her body pressed against mine, the warmth of her skin holding me hostage. I might as well be chained to the bed. I'd like to tie her up. That would be . . .

"Oh God," she cries, snapping up out of my arms. "We're in bed together."

"We've slept together lots of times," I say but know in my gut last night was different.

"We aren't kids," she says, getting up and straightening her clothes.

"You had a lot to drink," I say, trying to calm her down, not liking one bit how upset she is at the thought of us in bed together. "We talked and just fell asleep."

"I remember. But this," she snaps, waving her hand toward the bed, "this is how mistakes happen."

Feeling my jaw tense, I step closer to her and ask, "How do you know it would be a mistake?"

Her mouth falls open slightly, shocked at my forwardness. She really has no idea. "Because I'd be doing it in part to hurt Luke. I'd be using you to hurt him."

"What if I don't care?" I ask, daring her a little.

"You'd care."

The only thing I care about at the moment is her. Screw the code, fuck the rules. Being with her trumps everything else. "I know you won't care one ounce about Luke as soon as you let me kiss you. He'll be wiped from your memory. I can promise you that."

She stares at me for a minute, her blue eyes wide, her breasts rising and falling, and I bet her panties are soaked. There's chemistry between us that she can't deny. It's just not something either one of us has ever acknowledged out loud before. There are some people that you just know you'd have blow-your-dick-off great sex with. You meet them, and it's undeniable. There are also people you meet, and you know you'll be friends forever. Skylar is both.

"Answer your phone," she says.

"What?"

"Your phone," she says, motioning to my nightstand. "It's ringing. Answer it."

I'd been too wrapped up in her to even notice the world around me. I reach for it, and Skylar heads right for the door. Damn it, just when we were getting somewhere.

Still staring at the door, I pick up my phone. "Jax, hey man, it's Luke."

"Luke, hey," I say, looking down at the bed I was just in with the girl he shared his life with for the past decade. My eyes close, a heaviness sitting on my chest.

"Skylar there?"

"You know she is."

"Any chance she'll talk to me?" he asks.

"Doubt it."

He exhales. "She okay?"

"I'm watching out for her," I say, leaving out that I'm sleeping next to her, too.

"She tell you what happened?" he asks, his voice low.

"Not really."

"She ended it with me. I mean, ten years, and she just walks out. No discussion, nothing. I was so pissed off."

"Man, I really don't want to be in the middle of your drama."

"I slept with someone else," he says, and I can hear the regret thick in his voice. "Skylar knows."

I knew there was more to it than Skylar said. Luke is a good dude. I wouldn't expect something like this from him. "I'm surprised you still have your dick."

"That's the thing. I wish she'd been angry, but man, I will never forget the look in her eyes. The hurt. I fucking crushed her. I don't know that I'll ever forgive myself for doing that to her."

"Then why do it?"

"I was upset, and Skylar . . . she's . . . my first, the only woman I'd ever been with," he says, clearly ashamed or embarrassed about that fact. "I don't know, man. I just lost it for a little while. I need her to forgive me."

I listen to him for what feels like forever, my gut twisting more and more as he talks about how much he loves her, wants her back. By the time I hang up with him, I need a good, stiff drink. I'm not conflicted about Skylar, how I feel about her, what I want, but rolling over Luke to get it, that's against all the rules. But I've never been great at following the rules.

Walking down the stairs, I see Skylar in the kitchen, cutting up some fruit for breakfast. I usually wake up and look out at the water, but nothing beats her standing in my kitchen. This is what I want, to wake up with her here, and not as a houseguest. Friendship is important to me, but how I feel about Skylar is more important. It sucks, but if I have to lose a friend to gain her, then that's the price I'll pay.

She's worth it.

Her eyes catch mine, and I say, "That was Luke."

Slowly, she puts the knife she was using down, pushing her food away from her slightly. I wasn't about to keep his call a secret from her. She deserves to know. If she does end up with me, I don't want it to be because I played dirty and kept things from her. I mean, it can be because I like it dirty, but in the bedroom, not in our friendship.

"He told me what happened," I say.

Immediately, she heads toward the stairs, her head down, her body rigid, her movements quick, like she's on a mission.

"Skylar," I say, gently reaching out toward her, but she won't let me touch her.

"Let me go, Jax," she says. "I don't want to think about it."

"Luke is my friend, and he would agree with me. He's a fucking prick for doing that to you," I say.

Her eyes stare daggers at me. "No rule about how long you have to wait to screw someone else after a breakup?"

I'm in trouble. She's in "all men are assholes" mode. *Threat level red.* Someone should hoist the red flag up on the beach, warning hazardous conditions ahead.

"And if you're going to tell me that I broke up with him, so he's free to do whatever he wants, I don't want to hear it."

"Okay," I say, holding my hands up in peace.

"I really wish he wouldn't have told you. It's so embarrassing."

"Why be embarrassed by someone else's bad choices?"

"In my apartment, of all places," she says, her head hanging down. "I'd asked him to return my key. When I got home, he was in bed with another woman."

Luke left that part out. I can't believe he'd do that. Honestly, he's a good guy, but there's no excuse for that. I don't care how hurt he was, or if he was drunk off his ass. That's just cruel. That's why she came back to Waterscape when she did. That must've been the night before I picked her up at the airport.

"How am I ever going to sleep in that bed, in that apartment again?"

"You can always stay here," I say, meaning here in my house, but first things first. "In Waterscape."

She tilts her head. I'm sure she's unable to make any life-altering decisions right now. "I always thought us being each other's only was special," she says. "I guess he saw it as a handicap."

"Skylar?"

"Maybe that's why he never proposed. He wanted to test drive some other women first."

I'm not touching that comment with a ten-foot pole.

Gentleman's Rule—*Sometimes the best course of action is to let your woman vent!*

CHAPTER SIX

SKYLAR

Waterscape doesn't have a city ordinance on the style or color of the buildings and houses, but most of the town's center consists of white buildings with balconies and porches. The streets are wide, the sidewalks pressure washed, and there's not a speck of trash on the ground, even on race day.

The Jingle Run starts at the tourist building at the town's center and winds its way through the shops, restaurants, and galleries that the area is famous for. There's a Santa crawl for babies, and a one-mile race, which we are doing today. I haven't run in forever. The wintry weather in Chicago isn't conducive to outdoor exercise, and I'm not much of a gym person. I'm thankful that this run isn't along the beach. There is no way I'd be able to finish, something about running on the sand is ten times harder than running on the pavement.

Plus, Maci has me wearing this ridiculous Christmas tree costume. She and Malcolm are Mr. and Mrs. Claus, and the twins are little elves. It's the first time one of the guys has ever dressed up. Guess he's officially pussy-whipped. Jax isn't even wearing red or green. He's in running shorts and a white t-shirt. Everyone else has on cute little hats, red and white striped knee socks. Not me. I've got a green hood over my head with a huge star on it. Maci even went so far as to string battery operated lights off of me.

I'm not going to complain. Her theatrics lifted my mood after Luke's call to Jax this morning, reminding me of what I walked in on just a few days ago.

"How am I supposed to run in this?" I ask Maci, adjusting some of my bulbs.

"You look adorable," she says then looks to the guys. "Doesn't she, boys?"

Malcolm dutifully nods, while Jax covers his mouth, trying in vain to contain his laughter. His smile makes me smile. Jax is contagious that way. It's hard to be cross when he's got that smirk on his face.

We slept in the same bed last night. It was an accident on my part, but I'm not sure it was for him. He made it pretty clear this morning that he'd like to do more than sleep. Would serve Luke right if I fucked his friend after what he did. Jax didn't seem put-off by the idea, either, which surprises me. There's got to be some rule against banging your friend's ex! He and Luke aren't as close as they once were just with the distance and everything, but he'd risk their friendship for a roll between the sheets with me?

It doesn't really matter. I'm not the revenge sex type. If Jax ever ended up in my bed, it would have to be about more than sticking it to Luke.

We all take our places at the starting line. In the past, Maci and I would run together, but I know she'll be staying beside her little family this morning. That's the way it should be, and it makes me happy.

"You're not quite a Sequoia," Jax whispers in my ear.

I bust out laughing right as the buzzer sounds, starting the race. Everyone whizzes by me, the sound of jingle bells on running shoes echoing in my head. I try to run, but the stride of my legs is confined by my tree trunk. I'm moving at roughly the speed of a senior citizen in a walker.

The fact that I'm laughing so hard at myself isn't helping my situation. Maci looks back at me, snapping a picture of me on her phone. That's a good friend for you, the ones that have all the blackmail photos. She pats Malcolm on the shoulder, motioning toward me. The last thing I need is to draw more attention to myself.

"Go," I yell out. "I'll meet you at the finish."

"I got her," Jax calls out to them, then before I know what's happening, he hoists me up over his shoulder.

"Jax, put me down," I laugh as he starts walking the race. My bulbs are flying off left and right, leaving a little trail behind us. "You aren't a lumberjack. Plus, it's a full mile!"

"Smile!" someone says, and Jax angles me toward a camera, one of a local newspaper reporter, who says, "I see the caption now: Guy Gets His Tree."

I give Jax a light smack. "We're losing!"

He laughs and starts back walking again. The crowd is laughing and pointing at us. I know I'm beet red, but I give a few little waves in between hiding my face in my hands. Jax glances over his shoulder. "Doing okay back there?"

"I should be asking you that," I say. "I had all that fruit this morning."

He jiggles me a little. "Light as a feather."

"Liar." Playfully, his hand smacks my butt. "Jax Teigan, what on Earth has gotten into you?"

"'Tis the season," he says.

"For ass smacking?"

Gently, he puts me down. When my feet hit the pavement, his eyes are right on mine, his head tilted down. "For letting others know how we feel about them," he says.

How he feels about me? How is that? I'm a chicken. I'm not going to ask. He simply flashes me that panty-dropping smile of his then whisks me off my feet again, only this time I'm cradled in his arms like he's carrying me over the threshold.

Only it's not a threshold like I wanted for years, but a finish line we are heading for. We don't say anything else to each other while he carries me. Instead, I simply rest my head on his shoulder, admiring him. He really is a handsome man, but it's more than the sexy stubble on his face or his killer blue eyes.

It's his honesty. He feels something for me, and he says it.

No games. No wondering.

The entire crowd starts screaming as we approach the finish line. Bells are chiming, and fake snow falls all around us. He carries me across, giving me a sexy smile.

"Think we got last place," I whisper.

But inside I feel like I just might have won something else—his heart.

～

WHAT DO YOU do when you suspect the friend of your ex wants to get in your panties?

You hide, of course.

That's why as soon as we got back to Jax's house, I came out to the beach to take a walk, needing to clear my head, my heart, and my libido. I have a broken heart, there's no denying that. I'm attracted to Jax, there's no denying that, either. There's also no denying the confusion in my head.

There's been something between Jax and me for as long as I can remember—something special. Something that I didn't even share with Luke, and we're just starting to get back to that.

That friendship.

What bullshit that is. Just because you've never had sex or kissed someone, that doesn't mean you are "just friends." It's the desire that changes the friendship to more, not the act. The desire is definitely there, but I'm coming off a long-term relationship, and even if I wasn't, would I want to be the reason that Luke and Jax aren't friends anymore?

The answer to that is no.

Sitting down in the white sand and resting my head on my knees, I look down the beach. I have the place to myself. The beach is wide, the water vast, the sky unending, and I'm reminded how small I am, like a single grain of sand. So why does everything seem so huge right now?

I look out toward the horizon, where the blue sky meets the blue water. Two shades of the same color. That's the perfect way to think about Jax and me, we are two shades of the same color. Luke and I were like complementary colors. We worked well together, but Jax and I are the horizon, where he ends I begin, and vice versa.

The timing is just so wrong. I'm not ready for anything serious right now. I'm not ready for anything meaningless, either. The only thing I know is that it's Christmas, and I want to be happy.

Jax makes me feel happy.

Maybe it's that simple?

CHAPTER SEVEN

JAX

IN WAR AS in love, there are rules of engagement. You have to know when to strike, know when to wait, know when to go in guns blazing.

Skylar is all alone on the beach. She looks beautiful sitting there in the white sand, but she's staring at the water like she's searching for something. Now is not the time to go in full throttle. Now's the time to wait. I'd say most, if not all, women like to be pursued, but there's an art to it. Too much and you come off pussy-whipped. Too little and she won't feel desired. Both are equally dangerous. So I've got to play this right.

If I'm going to do something, I'm going to do it right. Some guys just don't know how to love a woman. They're either too scared or too selfish to do the job right. I think that's why my rules have been successful. It's basically a how-to guide on love.

The Gentleman's Rules to loving a woman are simple. Here are a few:

Gentleman's Rule—Make her feel desired.

She should never walk in a room without you acknowledging her. I'm not talking about glancing up from your phone, either. Get up off your ass, and give her a hug and a kiss. I don't care if you're busy or working. It takes less than a minute and will make her whole day. This is one of the smallest changes any couple can make in their relationship and reap huge benefits.

Gentleman's Rule—Notice her.

It's great to notice when she gets her hair done or has on a new outfit, but that's not what I'm talking about. I'm talking about noticing the little subtleties about her. Does she bite her lip when she's stressed or perhaps when she's horny? Does she stir her coffee before she drinks it? These are little clues she's giving you about her mood. If she usually stirs her cup three times, and one morning she's been stirring it for five minutes straight, then you know she's off, and you can try to help. Which brings me to number three.

Gentleman's Rule—Make her life easier, not harder.

Life is hard enough on its own, so if you can do something small each day to ease her load, why not do it? I'm not talking about big things, either. Women appreciate little details. They want to feel connected to you. Men, we want to have sex, lots of sex. Women want the connection first. How do they feel connected? By feeling understood. You don't even have to get it right all the time. Just try, and you'll be rewarded.

I think I've got the first two down with Skylar, but that last one is a little trickier. Her life would probably be easier right now if I didn't pursue her, but I just can't help myself. Waking up with her this morning sealed the deal. I need another fix.

Other than her dimple popping out, she didn't respond to my carrying her over the finish line. We spent the rest of the day hanging out in town with Maci, Malcolm, and the twins. Skylar made sure to have at least one body between us at all times. I suppose you could think that's her way of turning me down, but I know it's her way of cooling herself down. The attraction between us is that obvious, and I'm sure she doesn't want Maci asking questions, either.

The sun is starting to set. If she doesn't come inside soon, I'll go get her, but for now, I turn on the Christmas tree lights. They must call to her because within five minutes, she's walking through the door with a surprised look on her face.

I'm in the kitchen starting dinner. Not all bachelors are inept in the kitchen. My publishing house has asked me to do a gentleman's cookbook, but I'm not ready for that. I'm not inept, but being able to make five dishes successfully doesn't make me ready to pen a cookbook, either.

Tonight's dinner is a simple Alfredo pasta. I don't have the stuff for a salad or garlic bread to go with it, but Skylar doesn't seem to mind. I'm not sure which is thumping harder, my cock or my heart.

"Smells good," she says, directing her eyes to the pot and not to me.

"I have your mom to thank for that," I say. My mom was a waitress my whole life and couldn't cook a damn thing. "If not for your mom, I might have starved."

"She misses cooking. It's hard for her now," Skylar says.

"She looked really good last time I saw her," I say.

"Even so, they are only allowed refrigerators and microwaves in their rooms."

"She always made Christmas cookies and gingerbread houses with us this time of the year," I say, plating the pasta.

"My house never stood up," she says, finally making eye contact with me. "But then somehow the next day, it would always magically be put together."

She's on to me. Her mom snuck me back in for years to fix the disasters that were Skylar's gingerbread houses. I'd build it, and her mom would make it beautiful.

"Must've been Christmas magic," I say, as she rolls her eyes at me and takes a bite.

The Christmas season loses some of its magic as we get older. It tends to become busier, more about parties and gifts than the spirit of the season. I think it happens as soon as we discover that Santa Claus isn't a bearded dude sneaking down our chimney. The shift is natural, but I feel the magic this year. It has everything to do with the woman sitting across from me. Hers is a Christmas spell, and I'm thoroughly under it.

"I was thinking we should stay in tonight, maybe watch a movie," I say.

Let's be honest. *Watch a movie* is code for *let's have sex*. The only problem is, I'm not sure Skylar realizes that.

I catch her mid-bite, and she smiles, trying to chew quickly. She covers her mouth. *"The Polar Express."*

"Isn't that a cartoon?" I ask. She smiles, confirming my suspicion. That's all it takes to win me over—her smile—that little dimple of hers. Flash me a smile, and I'll do anything she wants. God, I'm easy.

I make her promise that if I can't find it, we'll watch some action flick instead, so after dinner and cleaning up, I make a quick check of my smart TV. Of course, it's right there ready to be streamed.

We settle in for movie night. For Skylar that meant a change of wardrobe, now wearing a pair of sweatpants and a baggy t-shirt that looks ten sizes too big. She's got funny looking socks on her feet, and all I want to do is pull her to me, to find out how it would feel to finally have her next to me, and not on accident. Instead, she's a good foot away from me on the sofa.

She watches the movie, and I watch her. She knows all the words to the songs and one song about hot chocolate makes her do a little dance. I really can't tell you what the movie was about. I can tell you Skylar's reactions to it, when she laughed, when she cried. How many times she nuzzled down deeper into the sofa cushions. I could watch her all night.

"I love that part," she says. "At the end, with the bell."

"I have a theory about all those elves," I say. "I think Santa and Mrs. Claus have been busy."

"You're terrible."

"Think about it," I say. "It's cold up there in the North Pole. Nothing to do. You've got to do something to stay warm."

She throws me a look, trying not to laugh. "Only you could turn Santa and Mrs. Claus into nymphos."

"Why else do you think he's so happy all the time?"

She tosses a pillow at me. "And that rosy complexion!"

I laugh. "Now you're getting it."

She giggles. "Maybe that's your next book. You can research how Mrs. Claus became Mrs. Claus. Where did they meet? Was their first kiss under mistletoe?"

"Sounds like a bestseller."

"The importance of the first kiss," she says. "I'd say there's a rule or two about that."

"You might be on to something."

"I should've known Luke and I weren't meant to be based on our first kiss alone," she says, shaking her head.

Must not have been great, but she's not going to tell me. That's fine. I don't want to know. I don't want to think about her lips on another man's, much less a friend of mine.

"The first kiss is important. The most important. It sets the stage for everything else. You can tell a lot about a guy by how he kisses," she says.

I should be taking notes. She's right. This is good stuff for the next book. "Really?" I ask, my eyes on her mouth.

Slowly, her tongue glides across her full, pink lips. "Is he slow and deliberate? Like he has the whole thing planned out? Or does he just grab you, wild and free?"

It works both ways. You can tell from the first swipe of a woman's tongue if she's going to be good in bed or not. My eyes on hers, I say, "The same is true for women."

She leans in closer and asks softly, "What would my kiss tell you?"

My lips hovering over hers, I whisper, "It would tell me you want this, no matter the consequences." She comes even closer, her breath mingling with mine. "That you've thought about being with me as much as I've thought about being with you."

She pulls her bottom lip between her teeth, whispering, "Just one kiss."

I've wanted to know how she tastes since I was sixteen years old, but if she thinks I'm going to settle for just one, she's got another thing coming. I don't mind playing dirty if I have to. She never specified where that one kiss had to be. Her mouth, her tits, that beautiful ass of hers—the possibilities are endless. Christ, I'd like to pull down those sweatpants and run my tongue along her pussy.

Instead, I look to her eyes then to her mouth, her lips slightly parted. Her eyes close. Fuck, the things I want to do to her. I could yank her on top of me, let her feel my hard cock between her thighs. I could slide my finger under the waistband of her sweatpants and feel how much she wants me, all the while not kissing her, not giving her the one thing she asked for, making her want me more. I could play like that with her.

I could kiss her on the forehead, get to my feet, and leave her wanting more. If she were any other woman, I might, but I want her too much to play games.

Gentleman's Rule—Boys play games. Men get down to business.

Pushing her hair off her shoulder, I lean in, the sweet smell of her skin calling to me. There's a spot on her neck that I used to stare at while we "studied" back in high school, and I always wondered what it would be like to kiss her there, if it would make her toes curl.

As soon as my warm breath touches the delicate skin of her neck, she trembles. "Jax," she breathes out.

I cup her cheek in my hand, and her eyes open. "I can't just kiss you once," I say, my voice giving away my emotions. "It won't be enough."

Her breath hitches, then before I know it, her lips are on mine. This is a first. I've never had a woman kiss me first, at least not like this. I know she needed this to be her decision. Quickly, I take control, pulling her into a straddle on my lap. My tongue meets hers, and her body melts into me. Winding my hand in her hair, I urge her closer, deepening our kiss. A sweet moan falls from her lips. Her hands grip my shirt, pulling me tighter. We seem unable to get close enough. It's the perfect mix of slow yet hard.

This isn't the kiss of friends. This isn't the kiss of lovers. This is the kiss you have when you are both, when you mean everything to each other.

Her hands slide to my face as we slow. She plants a couple sweet kisses on my lips, leaning her forehead against mine. I've made a career of knowing women—what they want, what they need, what they think. But I'm a fraud, because I've got no idea what Skylar's thinking right now.

I lean back, and her eyes open. She's in my lap, framed by the white lights of the Christmas tree, making her look like an angel. Moving a stand of hair from her cheek, I ask, "What did that tell you?"

A little smile forms on her red lips, and she says, "Everything I need to know." Grinning, I pull her to me again, giving her a soft kiss. Her fingers roam my face. "I don't want to think about what this means," she whispers, her eyes closing. "I just want to feel good."

"I can do that," I say, smirking at her.

She laughs, and I pull us down on the sofa together so her head is resting on my chest. Gently, I play with her hair. I already know what this means. At least for me, this means everything.

CHAPTER EIGHT

SKYLAR

My body shivers, and I pull at the blanket, realizing I'm not in bed. Opening my eyes, I'm alone on the sofa, a blanket draped over me. Jax must've done that. For the second night in a row, we slept next to each other. I hope he doesn't make a big deal of what happened. I've had enough big deals the last few weeks.

That kiss is at the top of that list.

I've never been kissed like that. Never.

Touching my lips, I close my eyes, remembering how soft his lips were, how his chest felt under my hands, the way my body coiled around his on the sofa. Suddenly, I'm not cold anymore.

"Morning," Jax says, bending down and kissing me on the forehead.

We're doing forehead kisses now? That's very couple-like of him.

"Glad you're up," he says. "We need to get going."

"Going where?"

He flashes me that smile. The one he gets when he's up to something, which seems like every day. "It's just a few days before Christmas," he says. "We've got things to do."

"Like?"

Suddenly, he pulls me into his arms, giving my booty a healthy squeeze. "It's a surprise."

"Jax, I think we . . ."

He holds his finger up to my lips. "We're not thinking, remember? We're just making you feel good."

JAX SMIRKS AT me from the driver's seat. He won't tell me where we're going. He won't tell me what we're doing. He even tried to get me to put a blindfold on, but that wasn't happening. Waterscape isn't that big, so he can't keep the secret for long. As soon as we take the turn toward the assisted living center, I know.

"You're taking me to see Mom," I say. "I was planning on seeing her today."

"Not exactly," he says, pulling into a parking space.

"What do you mean, not exactly?" I ask.

He doesn't answer, instead opening my car door. I head toward the front entrance, but he places his hand at the small of my back, directing me to another door.

"All visitors have to sign in," I say, motioning to the front entrance.

"They know we're coming," he says.

"You're being very cryptic," I say, giving him a smile.

He stops outside a door, leans over, and softly kisses my lips. "Don't cry, okay?"

"Why would I . . ."

He opens the door, leading into the massive kitchen. My mom's sitting in her wheelchair. She must be having a bad day. When she's feeling really good, she can sometimes go without her chair. My mom is beautiful. I guess all daughters think that about their mothers. She's got natural blonde hair that curves just right at the ends and her skin always looks sun-kissed. She looks like the California beach girls you used to see in old movies. Even at her age, she could give those young girls a run for their money.

She's sitting in front of a steel countertop and spread in front of her are cuttings boards, cookie cutters, and every kind of Christmas sprinkle imaginable.

Jax leans over and whispers in my ear, "I just thought we should return the favor for all the years she baked with us."

Tears streaming down my face, I wrap my arms around his neck, hugging him tighter than I've ever hugged another human being before.

"Do I get one of those?" my mom asks, holding her arms up. I start to head her way, and she teases. "I saw you the other day. I was talking about Jax."

We both give her huge hugs, and I get my first good look at everything on the table. The cutting boards have suction cups, the utensils all have non-slip handles. Even the cookie cutters have extra wide handles. Everything looks like it was especially designed for my mom.

"You did all this?" I ask Jax.

He just shrugs like it's no big deal. "I just made a call to the director to ask. I wanted you two to have a nice day together."

"You're not staying?"

Giving me a wink, he says, "I need to do a little last-minute shopping."

Not for me, I hope. I don't need anything else. He's given me the most wonderful gift today. "Stay," I say, reaching for his hand.

"You must," my mom says. "Who's going to fix Skylar's gingerbread house if you leave?"

"I knew it was you!" I cry out, poking his hard abs.

He rolls up the sleeves on his shirt. "Okay, I'm in."

∼

TWO HOURS, THREE batches of cookies, and one gingerbread house later, I'd expect my mom to be wiped out and hurting, but instead she's out of her chair, plating cookies to pass them out. "Mom, take it easy," I say. "I don't want to wear you out."

She simply waves her hand at me. I look at Jax, who's shoving a cookie in his mouth. He's eaten more than he's made. Some things never change. "Why don't I clean up, and you can take your mom to pass them out?"

I push the wheelchair toward my mom, and she takes a seat, holding the cookies in her lap. "You two should take the gingerbread house home to enjoy," Mom says then points to the counter. "Skylar, baby, could you get those cookies over there?"

I go to grab them, but Jax beats me to it. "Thank you," I whisper.

"It was fun," he says.

Leaning in closer, I lower my voice even more. "Are you doing all this to get in my panties?"

Grinning, he says, "No, but that could be a nice bonus."

I lift my eyebrows to say "maybe so" then push my mom outside. It's slightly chilly today, but she doesn't seem to notice, and Jax has me so hot and bothered that the cool air feels good to me. Mom introduces me to one of the staff members, handing her a cookie, then we continue down the path.

The center really does resemble a country club. Everything is clean and crisp, freshly painted. The rooms look like little cabanas all nestled together. The facilities are first-class with exercise equipment, pools, and even classes throughout the day to help foster a sense of community. My mom loves it here, which eases my guilt a little about living so far away and being unable to take care of her myself. She insists that on her bad days she wouldn't want me to have to help her shower or get dressed, but I'd still like to do more with her than just help front the cost of this place. We talk almost daily when I'm in Chicago, but I miss her.

"Jax invited me to stay at his house Christmas Eve night," Mom says. "Said he'd hire a nurse if I needed one."

I stop pushing her. He doesn't even have an extra bed? I wonder what possessed him to ask, although knowing him, he'd go buy one. That might have been the shopping he wanted to do today. Still, it's incredibly thoughtful that he'd include my mom. He's a good guy. Cocky and arrogant, but still a good guy. "He didn't mention it to me."

"It was sweet he offered," she says. "But they have a church service here in the morning and a huge breakfast. I don't want to miss that."

"How about we pick you up on Christmas Day?" I ask. "And you can come over. Maci, Malcolm, and the kids are supposed to come by later that night. Their parents, too. Then we can bring you back here."

"Jax suggested the same thing after I turned down his invitation to stay at his house," she says, giving me a look, like she's seeing right through me.

We pass a group of people, and Mom passes out more cookies. "How about Luke? He coming in for Christmas?"

As far as my mom knows, my surprise trip was just that. A surprise trip home, not a mad dash away from Luke. I push her over by a bench and take a seat.

Luke? I haven't thought about him all day. I certainly wasn't thinking about him last night on the sofa with Jax. It's strange for him not to be occupying space in my mind, or in my heart, for that matter.

"Mom, I . . ."

"Broke up with Luke," she says, finishing my sentence. "I know." My jaw drops. How did she know? Did someone tell her? "On your birthday," she says. "I've been waiting for you to tell me."

My head hangs, embarrassed about how everything went down, and ashamed that I haven't shared this with her. "I'm sorry I didn't tell you sooner. I didn't want you to worry about me."

"I knew," she says. "The morning after your birthday when we talked. I could hear it in your voice. You were trying to be so brave, so strong."

"It was rough for a few days, but I'm really okay."

"Know that, too," she says. "Jax?"

"I don't know what I'm doing," I say.

"That's good," she says.

"No, Mom. No, it's not," I say, getting to my feet and starting to pace. "Luke and I are through. I know that, but Luke and Jax aren't through. I don't want to come between them. Then there's Jax. He lives here, and I don't. I've been thinking about moving back, but who knows? And I don't know what he wants or expects from me. I thought I was ready to get married and have kids, and now I'm single, and have to start over with someone else."

"With Jax," she says simply.

"Yes, Jax," I say. "And I . . ." My rant stops as I realize what I just said. *I want to start over with Jax?* Did I really just say that? "That's not what I meant."

Mom reaches for me, directing me back to the bench and placing her hand on top of mine. Looking around, I notice some red poinsettias placed for decoration. Everything looks picture perfect, like it's there for a reason, a purpose. Have I been brought home this Christmas for a reason?

"There was always a spark between you and Jax. You and Luke, I never understood that," my mom says.

"Mom?" I cry out. "You love Luke."

"I do. And you always loved him, too," she says. "But there's love and then there's *love*. Jax would take a bullet for you. Luke would push you out of the way. There's a difference."

She takes a bite of a cookie, letting that sink in. "Why didn't you ever say that before?"

"Because what you had with Luke was safe, steady. That's what some people want. Others want the passion, but that kind of love can be dramatic. Each person has to decide what they want in their life."

"What if you want both?"

"Jax," she says.

CHAPTER NINE

JAX

"You're a total man!" Skylar cries playfully, placing her hand on my chest, a fake attempt to hold me back. We weren't home two seconds before I pinned her to the door, kissing her neck. "All you think about is sex!"

"I didn't say a word about sex," I say, leaning back in, letting my fingers roam up her thighs, feeling her quiver beneath my fingertips. "But I believe that's the second time you've brought it up today. Just now, and there was something earlier about me getting into your panties."

She hooks her fingers in the belt loop of my jeans, pulling my hips into hers. "You trying to tell me you've never thought about me and you?" she asks.

"Thought about, dreamt about, fantasized about, beat off to it," I say, kissing her neck.

"You're bad," she whispers.

"You never," I whisper, unbuttoning her jeans, "thought about me touching you?" She trembles underneath my touch as my fingers slip under her panties. "Tell me, Skylar."

"Your mouth," she says, kissing me then gently biting my bottom lip. Fuck! "I've thought about you kissing me all over."

Gentleman's Rule—When your woman asks for something in bed, comply—you'll be glad you did.

Lifting her, she wraps her legs around my waist, my cock finding his home between her thighs. My hands on her ass, I head toward the sofa. "Wait!" she whispers, looking toward the front door. "I heard something."

"It's nothing," I say, leaning in to kiss her again, but she hops down off me just as a loud banging starts on my front door.

"Told you," she says, fixing her hair and clothes.

I try to stop her. "It's probably just the postman delivering a package."

She playfully swats my hands. "Answer it." I motion down to my very hard dick. There is no way to hide him at the present moment. Smiling, she rolls her eyes. "I'll get it."

The knock comes again, and I blow out a deep breath. Skylar opens the front door to a flurry of red hair. "Thank God you're home," Maci says, stepping inside, a twin on each hip. "I need your help. Of course, I tried calling, but you never have your phone on these days."

"Everything alright?" Skylar asks.

"Harper, Parker," Maci says, putting them down. "Go look out the window at Uncle Jax's pool, but don't go outside."

Skylar tussles their hair as they run past her. They each give me a high five. They're only four, but they are fast little suckers, running across the room to the sliding glass door to take a look outside.

I step closer to Maci and Skylar. Maci looks over my shoulder at the twins then lowers her voice to a whisper. "We bought them this outdoor playhouse for Christmas, and I just got an email that it's been recalled!" She pushes on her eyes a little bit. "They're four, so they are all about Santa. I can get another kind, but I need to drive to Pensacola to get it. Malcolm's waiting on me. Can you please watch the twins for me? I'd ask my parents or Malcolm's parents, but they went to some music show or something together. Please, I wouldn't ask if it wasn't an emergency."

Skylar looks back at me. She seems as disappointed as I am about this turn of events. "Sure," I say.

"Thank you," Maci says, rushing to kiss her kids on top of the head. "Aunt Skylar and Uncle Jax are going to play with you this afternoon. I'll be back later." Then she mouths "thank you" to us and heads out.

"Wait," I call after her. "Do they nap or anything?"

"Not anymore," she calls out before hopping in her car.

"Oh shit," I mumble under my breath. "No nap."

∾

MY HOUSE IS great, but it's not exactly kid friendly. I don't have kids' toys. They got scared playing hide and seek. It's too chilly to use the pool, and Maci is very strict about the use of technology to babysit her kids—so no television and no video games.

Skylar and I brought them outside to build Waterscape's version of a snowman—a sandman.

No snow, no problem. The kids wanted their Uncle Jax to make them a snowman. We've got sand. We've got water. One sandman, coming right up.

It's actually not that hard. You use many of the same principles when building a sand castle. First, you collect some wet sand, gather it in your hands, squeezing out as much water as you can, then cover it with dry sand. Make various sizes, stack them up, use whatever shells, seaweed, or driftwood you can find on the beach to decorate. Boom! A sandman.

We've been out here for hours. Harper loves to build, put them together, and make them "cute," while Parker likes to crush them. It's the four-year-old version of war of the sexes.

"Stop it," Harper cries, crawling into my lap.

"Parker," I say, taking his hand. "Why don't you try building something instead of destroying everything?"

"No," he says, plainly. "This is more fun."

Skylar cracks up laughing. I look up at her in her oversized sweater and shorts, her hair pinned on top of her head. She's enjoying this a little too much.

"I had a sand daddy, a sand mommy, and a sand baby," Harper

cries, hugging my neck. "And he smashed them."

"Help me," I mouth to Skylar.

Grinning she takes one of both their little hands. "Parker, let's help your sister fix her sand family, then we can bury Uncle Jax in the sand."

"Yay," he yells, immediately starting to make some more sand balls like I taught him.

She takes Harper's hand, and they start combing the beach, looking for things to decorate with. Skylar's smart, beautiful, sexy, funny, and now I see, even amazing with kids. How can one woman be that perfect?

"Have you seen snow?" Parker asks me.

"Sure have," I say.

"Do these look like snowballs?" he asks, holding up his ball of sand.

The kid is brilliant. I'd forgotten all about the sand ball fights we used to have as kids. Malcolm, Luke, and I used to pummel each other. It was the best time. The sand ball war when we were twelve was epic, lasting two days. Leaning over, I whisper in Parker's ear, telling him the game plan—the rules.

See, there are always rules.

Basically, I let him know that Skylar is our target and not to hit his sister. I stack up as many sand balls as his little hands can carry then get to my feet.

"Attack!" Parker yells, as I grab Skylar from behind, lifting her in the air slightly as Parker tosses the balls at her. He's little, so he's not throwing hard.

Skylar's laughing and screaming, and even little Harper grabs a ball to toss at her.

"Jax!" Skylar cries. "I'm going to get you."

"Reload!" I tell the kids as Skylar wiggles free from my arms.

She turns around, and I catch her, planting a kiss on her lips. Her hands go to my hair, and I lift her up a little. We can't get too carried away. There are children present.

"Mommy! Daddy!" Harper and Parker suddenly both yell.

Like she's in the military, Skylar leaps out of my arms and snaps to attention.

"We had so much fun with Uncle Jax and Aunt Skylar!" the kids say, hugging their parents.

"I see that," Maci says, her eyes wide.

Malcolm clears his throat. "Come on kids, let's go." He tries to take Maci's hand, but she yanks it away, heading in our direction. Malcolm's a few steps behind her, motioning for us to move a little farther away from the kids, where everyone can still keep an eye on them, but their little ears won't hear what's about to go down.

"How long has this been going on?" Maci asks. "Is this why you broke up with Luke?"

"What? No!" Skylar says.

"I thought you told me everything. I thought I knew you," Maci says. "But now I don't know."

"Maci," Malcolm says, placing his hand on her shoulders. "This isn't our business."

She shakes her head at me. "Jax, this has to be the most selfish thing you've ever done. I don't care what Luke did. You're hooking up with your best friend's ex!"

"This doesn't involve you, Maci," I snap, wrapping my arm around Skylar, who's now in tears.

Malcolm throws me a warning look. He may know I'm right, but he'll take up for his wife no matter how wrong she is. "Let's go, Maci," he says, but she shrugs him off again.

"We don't have to explain ourselves to you," I say, keeping my voice as even as possible.

"Yeah, you do. We are all friends. What do you think is going to happen when Luke finds out? Do you think we can all be friends after you betrayed him like this?"

Skylar's shoulders start to shake, and she's crying harder now. "I don't think we were all going to be friends after what he did to Skylar, anyway," I say.

"Oh," she says to me, throwing her hands up. "So just move in on his girl then."

"Please stop," Skylar says.

"Maci, that's enough!" Malcolm barks, and she throws her husband a death stare.

Dude just broke one of the cardinal rules.

Gentleman's Rule—*Your woman is right, even when she's wrong.*

"You should go," I tell them.

Malcolm nods, but Maci turns back to me. "Don't like what I have to say, so you're kicking us out?"

"I don't like that you're making Skylar cry," I say.

Skylar wipes her face a little. "I'm fine," she says.

"Jax, you don't like the truth," Maci counters.

"Here's the truth," I say. "You're the one being selfish right now. You're only thinking about how this is going to affect you. You don't care one bit about how happy Skylar and I are."

Skylar looks up at me, shock in her eyes. Did she not realize how damn happy she's made me the last few days?

"I am thinking about Skylar. She's coming off a breakup!" Maci says, snapping her fingers. "She can't just move on like that. Did it ever occur to you that she might need some time?"

"What would you know about it?" Skylar asks, finally getting in on the action. "You've only been with Malcolm, so please don't tell me how to act. If you found Malcolm in bed with another woman, you have no idea what you'd do. There are no rules for this."

"I know I wouldn't sleep with Jax!" Maci cries.

Malcolm and I look at each other, and we can't help but laugh. Women are crazy sometimes. Skylar looks up at me, and starts giggling herself. She raises an eyebrow at Maci, who rolls her eyes. "No offense, Jax."

"None taken," I say. "I wouldn't sleep with you, either."

Skylar reaches out and takes Maci's hands. "Jax and I aren't sleeping together."

"Yet!" I tease.

"Not helping," Skylar scolds me playfully then turns back to Maci. "I'm actually glad you know."

"Watch out," Malcolm says. "They'll be talking about you now, Jax."

Skylar says, "I know this is a shock, but . . ."

"I'm worried about you," Maci says quietly. "Luke is his friend. There's no way for this to end well."

The tears start falling again, and Skylar quickly walks off, heading back to my place. But I stand my ground on the beach, wanting to ram my fist into something.

Maci turns to me. "Do you expect us to keep this from Luke?"

"I didn't realize you were talking to Luke. I thought you were pissed at him for what he did to Skylar."

"I am!" she cries. "But he talks to Malcolm. Calling him every damn day in tears over losing her."

I look at Malcolm, his nod confirming that Luke isn't moving on from her. Can't say I blame him, I've never been able to truly move on from her, either. But I know Malcolm. He's a man of few words, and he keeps his nose out of other people's business. He won't say a word to Luke. He's not a liar, though. If Luke asks him directly, Malcolm would be honest, but Luke has no reason to do that. No reason to suspect that his friend and his ex can't keep their hands off each other.

"Doesn't our friendship mean anything to you?" Maci asks me.

"Does Skylar's mean anything to *you*?" I bark. "A friend sticks by you through thick and thin. They are there to help you pick up the pieces when you fall on your face, not just when you agree with them. I suggest you think about that!"

I give Malcolm a nod, hug the kids, then walk toward my house. I know how much Maci means to Skylar. How much girlfriends mean to each other. This is bad.

It's time for damage control.

Hurrying inside, I expect to find Skylar packing her stuff to leave or face-first on the sofa in tears. Instead, she's standing in front of the gingerbread house we made, her fingers gently touching the candy decorations. I watch her for a moment, how delicately she moves. I can almost see the thoughts in her head, the doubt hanging over her like a dark cloud.

She knows I'm there and says, "Maci's not wrong. We're going to hurt someone we both care about. And for what? A roll in the sheets? A few kisses?"

"This is way more than that," I say.

"How are we supposed to do this? Our friends don't even support us."

"Malcolm will be fine," I say. "Maci's only thinking about Maci right now."

"And we're just thinking about us."

"And it's about damn time," I say. "It should've been us at prom. We should've been college sweethearts. We should've been each other's first." I reach out and take her hand. "The past ten years should've been mine."

"Oh fuck me," Maci says, coming through the sliding glass door. "If you don't sleep with him after he says something like that, then I will."

Skylar starts laughing through her tears. Maci comes over, and they hug each other. They don't fight often, and when they do, it usually doesn't last long. All their fights end the same way—like this—a long hug.

Maci pulls back and says, "I'm a bitch. I'll blame it on the pregnancy hormones. I'm sorry. It's not my place to judge."

Skylar takes my hand. "Believe it or not, this has nothing to do with Luke. I'm not trying to hurt him."

"But you know it will when he finds out," Maci says softly.

"I know," Skylar whispers. "Jax and I are taking things slow."

We are? Since when? Was it slow when I had her pinned against the wall earlier?

"I don't want you hurt again," Maci says to her. "And I know it's going to hurt you to hurt Luke this way."

"If there was any way not to hurt Luke, I'd do it," I say. "But . . ."

"You've felt this way about her a long time," Malcolm says, stepping inside, a kid in each arm. Maci turns to him. "Senior prom, he got drunk, told me everything. Still looks at Skylar the same way now."

Maci and Skylar both look at me with their jaws on the floor. Shaking my head at Malcolm, I say, "Dude, you say like fifty words a day, and you decide to spill that right now?"

Malcolm laughs, "Let's go home, Maci. Think we've done enough damage for one night."

A few hugs more, and they leave. I shut the door behind them. Things aren't perfect. I think that might take a little time. Maci said some things that really hurt. I know Skylar will act like she's fine, that none of it bothered her, but it's going to take some time.

I look over at Skylar. There's no telling what she is thinking. Does she think this is a mistake? Does she want to stop while we still can? Before anyone gets hurt?

"Well, that's the last time I babysit for her," Skylar jokes.

I run my fingers through her long brown hair. "You okay?"

She smiles and shrugs. "Maybe I should call Luke."

My heart misses a beat, maybe two. "You still love him?"

"Jax," she says, turning away. "Don't ask me that."

Fuck, I guess somewhere inside me I knew she did. It would be impossible for her not to. They haven't been apart very long, plus they spent a lot of years together. Still, it stings. No, it fucking burns like someone's taken a hot branding iron to my heart.

"I'm always going to love him. We shared a lot together," she whispers. "But that doesn't mean I want to be with him."

"But it might mean that you're not ready to be with someone else."

Her blue eyes hold mine. "If it were anyone else, you'd be right," she says, stepping closer. "But you're not just anyone else."

That time her words make my heart speed up. "What would you

say to Luke?"

"I don't know," she says. "Would it hurt you if I called him?"

Shit, fuck, damn it. Why do women ask guys questions like that? Men don't like admitting hurt under any circumstance, much less a hypothetical one. "I don't think you should worry about me." Good answer on the fly—my man card is still in good standing.

She leans her head on my shoulder. "Maybe after the holidays."

Breathing her in, I wrap my arms around her. "What was it you said about going slow?"

She giggles, and I feel her whole body smile in my arms. She tilts her head up. "You didn't know I was that good a liar, did you?"

"You little . . ."

She pulls me into a kiss. "Had you worried for minute."

CHAPTER TEN

SKYLAR

JAX IS NOTHING if not a gentleman. He didn't push anything with me last night. He kissed me a lot, held me close, but kept things light and fun. The more space he gives me, the more space he seems to be taking up in my heart, not to mention my bed.

That was the one thing he did assume last night. The other nights we'd slept together could be considered "accidents." We just happened to fall asleep, but not last night. Crawling into bed together last night was entirely intentional.

And holy hell, he sleeps in only his boxer briefs. I wonder if he usually sleeps naked, and only kept those on for my benefit? I woke up with his arm draped over me and his dick poking my ass. He's not even awake yet, and that situation is going on. Arching my back, I push against him. Even in his sleep, he groans. Men? Not even a state of unconsciousness reduces their libido.

God should've planned it better. Men wake up with hard-ons, and women wake up and have to pee. That's not exactly a good combo.

Wiggling out from under his arm, I quietly try to scoot out of his bed, but he mumbles, "Come back to bed."

"Just need a minute," I say, kissing his forehead, his eyes still closed.

The room is almost completely dark. He's got these shades on the windows to block out the sun. Unfortunately, they also block out the view. Looking over at Jax in bed isn't a bad view, either. He's kicked all the covers off. It's dark, but I can still make out the edges of his muscles, his hair messy from sleep.

He used to sleep at my house all the time when we were younger, but I've never seen him like this. He always had his clothes on back then. Sure, I've seen him on the beach shirtless in his board shorts, but this is something else. He looks so peaceful, vulnerable almost.

The last thing I want to do is hurt him. When I mentioned calling Luke, I could see the pain in his eyes, even though he wouldn't admit it. What the hell am I doing?

It's not often that I have no clue what I'm doing, but I'm completely clueless right now. Jax makes me feel good, so I'm going with it. It's Christmas, and I just want to be happy. All the drama surrounding my business and Luke will be waiting for me after the New Year.

Walking into his bathroom, I smile. My toothbrush and his are next to each other on the counter. It looks like we're living together, but I'm just a houseguest. Well, I guess I'm more than that. I hear a phone ring from the bedroom and know it's his cell. Mine's been turned off for days. I use the bathroom and brush my teeth, making sure to leave my toothbrush next to his, wondering if he notices simple things like that. If I were a betting woman, I'd wager that he definitely noticed my birth control pills sitting out on the counter next to my things. Like most men, he probably thanked God for that knowledge.

Slowly, I open the door, trying to be quiet since I know he's on the phone. I see him sitting up on the side of the bed, his back to me, allowing me to drool over his broad shoulders.

"I can't tonight," he says quietly. I move to go tell him to do whatever he needs to do, but then he laughs. "You miss me?"

Quickly and quietly, I close the door, realizing he's on the phone with another woman. One he's probably having sex with. One who he's not taking things slow or being a gentleman with. Suddenly, I feel the need to shower. I don't have a lot of experience with guys. Dated a few in high school, and in college before Luke and I got serious freshman year, but even then, I didn't like dating. If I'm honest, it's probably one of the reasons I stayed with Luke so long. I didn't want this feeling. I didn't want to wonder if a guy was playing with me. I didn't want to feel so unsure.

Maybe my mom was right, and I'm the type that likes a steady, safe relationship. Because this feeling in my stomach right now feels downright terrible.

Reaching into the shower, I turn the nozzle. Jax has some special system in his house where you don't have to wait for the water to heat up. The hot water is automatically hot when you first turn it on, so there's no reason for me to be waiting to step inside, still fully dressed in my sleep clothes.

I'm frozen, standing there. I've got no claim to Jax, none at all, but I know myself well enough to know that I can't be one of many.

"Thought you were coming back to bed," Jax says sleepily, opening the door a crack, but not enough to see me or for him to come in.

"I'm kind of awake now," I say, managing to keep my voice steady. This time he sticks his head in a little, realizing I'm not in the shower yet. When he sees I'm decent, he steps inside. "Booty call?" I ask.

His eyes dart to mine, saying, "She won't be calling again."

"Why is that?" I ask.

He places his hands on my waist. "I told her next time you might answer my phone, and you won't be nearly as cordial as I was." I wiggle free from his hold. "Skylar, it was . . ."

"Don't," I say. "Don't tell me it was nothing, or that it was *just sex*. Luke tried to sell me that same line of bullshit. I'm not buying."

"But it *was* nothing," he says with sincerity.

"Then I guess if I slept with Luke, it would be nothing."

"Don't even joke about that," he snaps.

His eyes look so hurt, his jaw so tense, that for the first time I realize how awful it must've been for him watching me with Luke all these years. If he cares about me at all beyond normal friendship, that must've been the worst kind of torture. His words from the other night flash in my head.

"It's the worst feeling in the world to watch someone you love with someone else, knowing no one could love her better than you."

"You were talking about me," I say. "The other night." Recognition shows in his eyes, and he nods. "I'm sorry," I whisper. "I shouldn't have said that about Luke."

He smiles a little, letting me know I'm forgiven. "There's no one else," he says.

Who Jax sleeps with shouldn't matter to me. The relief I feel in my heart shouldn't be there. My head knows I'm in so much trouble, but my heart just doesn't give a damn. Lightly, I kiss his lips.

"Didn't you want to shower?" he asks, his hands on the bottom of my shirt.

Okay, so I can count on one hand how many people have seen me totally naked in my whole life. Only one of those has seen me naked in the broad light of day, showing off all my goods, so this is a little unnerving. This is another reason why dating sucks. You have to get used to stuff like this with someone else.

"You first," I say.

That was a big mistake, because he just strips off his boxer briefs in one swoop, not shy at all, not one ounce of insecurity. Then again, he's a god, so what's he got to be nervous about? I will my eyes not to look down, but I can't look in his eyes, either.

He chuckles, and the next thing I know, he's picked me up, and I'm under the shower head, fully dressed, my pajamas soaking wet. "Oh my God," I say, unable to keep myself from laughing. "You are a lunatic!"

He splashes some water on me. "You wanted to shower, and it didn't look like you were going to get undressed anytime soon, so . . ."

"This is the only thing I have to sleep in," I say, throwing my hands up playfully.

"You can wear one of my t-shirts," he says. "Or sleep naked."

"I'm in the shower completely covered, and you think there's a chance in hell I'm going to sleep naked with you?" He laughs, placing his hands on either side of my face and kissing me. "Just shower and get out!" I say, feigning annoyance.

He steps under the nozzle, soaking his face and hair. When his back's to me, I seize the moment and slip off my wet clothes, stepping toward him and wrapping my arms around his waist, letting my naked body press into his. He jerks slightly then turns his head, trying to get a look at me, but I hold him to his spot, letting my hands roam the edges of his muscles. He lets me for a few moments then takes my hands, giving them each a kiss.

I inch back, letting him know it's okay to turn around. As soon as his eyes land on me, my nerves settle. Just the way his eyes slowly slide over my body makes my muscles clench.

"How'd I get so lucky?" he whispers.

"Guess you've been a good boy this year," I tease. "Want to join me on the naughty list?"

He shakes his head at my corniness. "I feel like I'm a kid in an expensive store, and I'm not supposed to touch," he says softly. "You're worth too much."

Wow! Just wow! That's all I can think.

"Just don't break me," I whisper, my voice cracking.

"Don't you know you're unbreakable?" he asks.

That might be one of the best things that anyone has ever said to me. To have someone believe in your strength means a lot. It actually makes you stronger. Jax being the one who believes in me that much makes me feel like I can do anything. With him beside me, I probably could, and if I faltered, he'd carry me across the finish line.

His fingers follow the path of the water across my collarbone. My body trembles. Just when I think his hand is going to drift lower, he cups my face and whispers, "I love you."

Um, what just happened? What did he say? I was ready for some serious foreplay, not serious declarations. Stunned, I step back, slipping and busting my butt on the shower's tile floor.

"Shit," he cries, kneeling in front of me. "Are you okay?"

My ass is fine. It's my heart that's a battered mess. I could've handled that more gracefully. He tries to help me to my feet, but I get up on my own accord. The only thing I've hurt is my pride and the moment. Reaching for the shower door, I make my getaway. I'm not exactly running away from him, but it's a fast walk, for sure.

"Skylar," he calls after me, turning off the shower and wrapping a towel around his waist. I'm out the bathroom door with his t-shirt over my head by the time he catches up with me. "That's not exactly how I thought that would go," he says, reaching for me.

I step back and say, "I'm not ready."

"I realize that now," he says, running his fingers through his wet hair. "I wanted you to know how I felt before things went further. It felt to me like the right time to say it. But what do I know? I've never said it to anyone before."

I fall on my ass again, only this time I land on the bed. He's never said that to a woman before? How's that possible? I'm his only? The only woman he's ever loved?

"You were my first love," I whisper but don't make eye contact.

He kneels, taking both my hands. His blue eyes look up at me, full of warmth. "I want to be your last," he whispers back.

Leaning my forehead on his, I close my eyes, knowing I'm not ready to say those words to another man, even if it's true. "Knowing the right time to say *I love you*," I say softly. "Is there a gentleman's rule for that?"

"There will be now," he says with a smirk. "And not while the woman is on a slippery surface will be rule number one."

CHAPTER ELEVEN

SKYLAR

It's time to do a little last-minute Christmas shopping. Jax opens my car door in front of the main shopping village in Waterscape, an open area that looks like something out of a magazine advertising beach living.

He smacks my ass, and I jump slightly. Most men might toss you a kiss on the cheek or a "later, babe," but not Jax. He pulls me into his arms, gently rubbing my booty cheeks. "You hurt yourself earlier."

"I'm fine," I say, planting a sweet kiss on his lips. I'm actually more worried about him. If I told someone I loved them, and they reacted like I did, I'd be crushed, but Jax is acting totally normal. "Are you?"

"It's Christmas. You're by my side. All's good."

"I'm talking about earlier," I say. "Are you okay?"

"Skylar," he says tenderly. "I love you. I didn't expect for you to say it back—although I didn't expect for you to fall on your gorgeous ass, either."

"Jax!"

"Look, I'm not going to hold anything back with you. I did that for a long time. I'm not going to do that anymore. It's that simple."

"This is anything but simple."

His lips land on mine in a sweet kiss. "Simple," he whispers. "Now finding the perfect Christmas gift for you, that requires a little more work."

"Don't buy me a gift," I say.

"I buy you a gift every year," he says.

"I know, but I left yours in Chicago," I say. "Along with everyone else's."

I'd been in such a hurry to get out of town that I left all my Christmas gifts behind. Mom will understand, so will Maci and Malcolm. I'd only planned on replacing gifts for the twins, but I guess I need to add Jax to that list. "I'm planning on shipping them to you guys when I get back to Chicago."

His arms cross over his chest, his blue eyes narrowing. "You're not going back to Chicago."

"Even if I decide to move back here, at some point, I will have to go back to Chicago."

He thinks about it for a second, and I can't help but smile. I can see him literally trying to devise a plan in his head where I wouldn't ever have to step foot back in the Windy City. Finally, he says, "Then I'll go with you."

This is one of many ways that Jax and Luke are like night and day. Luke didn't have a possessive bone in his body. I don't remember him ever being jealous. Luke was protective, but in a completely rational and calm way. I can already tell this isn't the case with Jax. He'll take defending my honor to the grave.

"Let's talk about it after Christmas. Right now, I have to get new gifts for Harper and Parker," I say, elbowing him gently. "And you."

"Can it involve you naked?" he asks.

Laughing, I say, "My ass is still sore from last time you saw me naked."

He pulls me tight to him. I can feel his dick pressing against my belly. He lowers his head into my neck, his breath sending tickles down my spine. "I'll kiss it and make it better."

I pull away, giving him a little wink and tease, "You better."

A huge grin on his face, he takes my hand for a second. "I'll meet you back here in an hour."

Smiling, I head toward the shops of the town center. Waterscape doesn't have any big chain malls or stores. You'd have to drive further inland for that. It's the day before Christmas Eve, and who wants to drive and fight that? So I've settled for the quaint boutique shops of Waterscape.

I look back over my shoulder and see Jax standing there, leaning against his car. It's as if he doesn't want to let me out of his sight, like if he does, this will all fade away. I throw him another smile and a wave before disappearing into the crowd.

Even though Waterscape is a small town, it's crowded during the holidays. We get a lot of people escaping the harsh winters of the north. I should know. I've done that a time or two myself. I've heard people say it doesn't feel like Christmas unless there's snow, or it's cold. I've spent Christmas in a blizzard, and I've spent it in a bikini. I have to say that Christmas only feels like Christmas when you're with the people you love. That's what makes the holiday special, not sweaters and hot chocolate.

Still, Waterscape has gotten on the hot chocolate bandwagon—a popup cart of frozen hot chocolate graces the sidewalk. Lights outline the stores, and garland streams across the pathways. Santa and his reindeer are at one end, greeting all the children. A smile graces my lips when I think about spending tomorrow with Jax, and then Christmas Day with Mom and our friends. It couldn't feel more like Christmas.

Last year, I vowed that I wouldn't spend another Christmas with Luke if we weren't engaged. I kept that promise. I didn't know then that I'd be spending it with another man, especially not one of his best friends. Life is funny sometimes—though I know there's nothing funny about this situation, or what's coming. It's inevitable that this will blow up in our faces. I just hope it's later rather than sooner.

I duck into a children's toyshop. I had superhero capes made for the twins this year, personalized with their initials and everything. Parker's is blue and red, and Harper's is pink and purple. I know they would've loved wearing them and chasing each other around. Too bad they are wrapped and still sitting on my coffee table in Chicago.

I've got to find something fantastic, but it looks like things are pretty picked over.

Bending down to look on a lower shelf, a slight pain hits my booty. That was not my best move this morning.

Jax *loves* me?

He actually said those words to me. It took Luke almost a year to say those words to me. When you break up with someone, you wonder if and when you'll find love again. It's much sooner than my crazy mind thought it would be.

The fact that he's never said it to any other woman, either—that makes it even bigger. The pressure of the word *love* didn't seem to faze Jax one bit. Love usually has strings attached, like commitment. Is that what Jax intended?

Toys! I'm supposed to be looking at toys.

Am I just a toy to him? Am I like all those Christmas gifts we can't wait to get as kids, and two days later are cast aside?

That can't be. I know Jax better than that. Whatever this is between us, it's serious to him.

That's ever scarier than being his plaything.

I just ended serious. Do I want to go back to that? And so soon?

Presents for the twins! Focus.

Legos? Lincoln Logs? Tricycles? The twins have everything. What's an aunt to do? I'm definitely not resorting to clothes or putting money in their college fund. I won't be *that* aunt. The toy store ends up being a complete bust, so I grab myself a frozen hot chocolate, soak in some Christmas music, and hit the next store.

Art supplies, they have to have something. After twenty minutes of debating my options, I conclude that I'm too good a friend to buy Maci's kids something that she will have to clean up and will drive her nuts. I might as well buy them a drum set.

Having finished my drink, I toss some money in a charity bucket and am rewarded with a candy cane. Tearing off the wrapper, I realize I'm running out of time. They're too young for cash or gift cards. My eyes land on a store sign, and genius strikes.

A baby store!

Maybe they have something there for big brothers and big sisters, like a book, t-shirt, video, doll, or something. This could be perfect until I can get their "real" gifts sent to them. Although, if Jax has his way, I'm never going back to Chicago. I'm not sure about his hesitation. It's not as though I'd be going back to see Luke.

Tossing my candy cane in the trash, I push open the door and see the place is pretty empty. I guess last minute shopping for nursery furniture isn't big on Santa's list this year. A sales associate points me in the right direction. Bingo!

I load up on matching t-shirts and onesies for them and the baby, a couple books, and a video. Quickly, I pay and ask the sales lady to please gift wrap it for me. While I'm waiting, something catches my eye, and I walk to a display near the front window, the most beautiful white bassinet with pink ribbons waiting there. Maci's so lucky to have a son and a daughter—I wonder what she wants this time. I'm sure Harper wants a sister and Parker, a brother.

I run my fingers along the ribbons. I wouldn't say my clock is ticking, but I definitely see kids in my future. Luke always talked about wanting a big family, but it always seemed like a distant plan for him. I pick up a sweet little pink onesie, holding it up. Are they really this tiny?

Looking down at my stomach, it seems impossible that a baby could grow in there. It shouldn't. I've seen Maci do it, and with twins. She carried them full term, too. We were all there when she delivered with Malcolm at her side—me, Luke, and Jax. I doubt it will be that way for their next baby, and if it is, will it be peaceful?

"Skylar?" I hear my name being called by a sweet voice. "I told you that was her."

My eyes land on the people that have been my second family, Luke's parents. I'm so stunned that I don't say a word, frozen still. They must hate me, but they've got huge smiles on their faces. Before I know it, they're hugging me tightly. Not exactly the reception I expected to get after dumping their son.

"We were just walking by and saw you through the window," his mother says before pulling back, raising an eyebrow at me. "Something you and Luke need to tell us?"

"What?"

She eyes the onesie still in my hand. I throw it down like it's a rag soaked in poison. "Oh, no, I'm here buying a gift," I say, holding my hand out to the sales associate bringing me my wrapped packages.

Is it me, or does his mom look disappointed?

"Luke didn't tell us you were coming," she says.

"Last minute," I say, wringing my hands together.

"Luke didn't come with you?" his dad asks.

A lump forms in my throat. It hits me like a ton of bricks. Luke hasn't told them we broke up. Why? Is he embarrassed by his behavior? Is he thinking he can win me back before having to let them know?

"Um, no, he's back in Chicago."

Both their brows furrow. It's not unusual for me to be in town without Luke. I do it for business all the time. The difference this time is it's just a few days before Christmas, and Luke didn't mention it to them.

Out of nowhere, Luke's dad taps on the front window and waves. "Look at that. There's Jax. The whole crew is here today." Jax smiles, but his eyes go straight to me. He heads inside the store.

A reunion in a baby nursery store—just what I was hoping for!

"Actually, I'm staying with Jax this trip," I say. "Maci's kids were sick."

Jax hugs them both then steps beside me, his hand going to the small of my back, and I take a step away. I throw him a look, trying to convey to him that they don't know about the breakup, but can tell he doesn't get the message.

"We were hoping Skylar was shopping for our future grandchildren," his mom says, patting my stomach.

By the look on Jax's face, he got *that* message loud and clear. His eyes narrow at me. Glaring, he says, "Skylar and Luke broke up."

It's like a bomb just went off. They look completely devastated. Their eyes are wide. Their mouths have fallen open, and Luke's mom looks like she's on the verge of tears. "What?" she cries, his father wrapping an arm around her.

How could you, Jax?

My heart breaks for Luke's parents. They don't deserve to find out this way. They are the sweetest people, and it's right before Christmas. They should've been told with more tact. The store attendant glances over at us.

"Let's step outside," I say, motioning with my arm and leading them to the door.

I throw Jax the bitchiest glare I can manage and tell him, "Give me a minute alone, please." I'm not sure what looks more rigid, his shoulders or his jaw. He doesn't like it one bit that I'm dismissing him, but he's done enough damage. Jax kisses Luke's mom on the cheek and shakes Luke's dad's hand before walking a few feet away and leaning against a white post. He's not within earshot, but I can feel his stare.

"Why wouldn't Luke tell us?" his dad asks.

"I don't know," I say. "It happened a few weeks ago. I'm sorry you had to find out this way."

"But you've been together so long," his mom says. "What happened?"

I won't badmouth their son to them. We have a lot of good memories. I will not tarnish that with the horrible way it ended. There's no need for them to know the gory details. It would only hurt them. Stepping closer, I take her hand and say, "I think you should hear that from Luke."

She nods, giving me a big hug. "You've been like a daughter to us. Can whatever happened be fixed?"

God help me, I don't have it in me to tell them "no," so I stay quiet, stealing a glance at Jax, who's seething a few feet away. I'm sure he'd rather I go on a rant about how there's not a snowball's chance in hell of that happening, but it's Luke's job to explain things to his parents, not mine.

"Let's not pressure Skylar," he tells his wife then turns to me. "I hope you have a Merry Christmas."

"You, too," I say, watching them turn and walk away. A few tears fall from my cheeks. When you date someone, you date their family. I was lucky in that respect. I loved both Luke and his family.

"Why didn't you tell them?" Jax asks, coming over to me.

"I had two minutes before you showed up," I snap. "And it took me almost that long to figure out that Luke hadn't told them."

Regret shoots through his eyes, apparently realizing he was an asshole. "Are you alright?" he asks tenderly, rubbing my shoulder.

Jerking away, I say, "With them, yes. But not with you. You had no right to do what you did."

"Skylar, you have no idea what it was like watching you with someone else all those years. When they assumed you and Luke were still together, I just didn't have it in me to hide my feelings about that anymore. I wasn't thinking."

"I would've told them," I say. His mouth opens in what I assume is going to be a lame apology, and I hold up my hand to stop him. "Let's just go home."

WE MAY BE in the sunshine state, but things stayed pretty icy between Jax and I the rest of the day. Staring down at his bed, I'm unable to climb under the covers. He's back on the sofa. Maybe I've grown so accustomed to feeling his warm body next to mine that I can't fathom crawling into that bed without him. Maybe I'm still angry at what he did.

Home?

That's what I said to him. I told him to take me home, and this is what I meant. I didn't mean Chicago or my apartment. I meant here, and it wasn't one of those slips of the tongues that happens when you're on vacation, and you refer to the hotel as home. No, I wanted to come back here, to a safe place, a place of comfort and love.

Grabbing a pillow and blanket, I head downstairs. Tiptoeing, I search the darkness, but I'm at the bottom of the staircase before I realize that Jax isn't on the sofa. The light isn't on in his office or any other room. Did he leave? He wouldn't just leave me here without telling me? Did I miss a note?

I head to the garage to see if his car is gone, and I see a light coming from underneath the door. Wonder what he's doing in the garage at this hour? He probably can't sleep, either, and I don't have the energy to have a big discussion with him right now. I turn around, heading to my original destination—the lone chair on his patio.

Placing my pillow down, I snuggle under the blanket, looking up at the stars. It's chilly, but I don't care. Jax and I used to sleep outside when we were kids, staring up at the night sky. Hopefully the galaxy can give me a fresh perspective. I look up trying to find the star, the one that will show me where I need to go. The one I need to make a wish on.

This season hinges on following a star, and I could use a little guidance from above right now. Every time I turn around, I seem to be upsetting someone—Maci, Luke, his folks, Jax. If only wishing on the right star could make things right for everyone.

So that's what I wish for—happiness for those I love.

Going left to right, I make my way through the stars, making the same wish—on the bright ones, on the faint ones, on the ones that are probably just satellites. Instead of counting sheep, I'm wishing on stars, but the result is the same, and I drift off to sleep, a wish on my lips.

∼

FEELING A LIGHT kiss on my lips, my eyes open. The morning sun is bright, signaling the beginning of Christmas Eve. "You're cold," Jax says, rubbing my arms a little. "What are you doing out here?"

Ignoring him, I say, "It's Christmas Eve." When we were kids, that meant making reindeer food to leave out and going to church. "Anything we need to do to get ready for tomorrow?"

"Need to wrap a few gifts and some food is being delivered, but that's it." He shakes his head. "You didn't answer my question. Why are you sleeping outside?"

"I didn't mean to fall asleep," I say. "I just came out here to think."

I sit up, the blanket falling from my shoulders, and a cold breeze hits me. Quickly, I lift it up on my shoulders and walk inside, Jax following me. I head upstairs to his bedroom. With each step I take, I feel emotions bubbling up inside.

He captures my hand, but I don't turn to him. "That was a shitty thing you did with Luke's parents yesterday."

"It was," he says, tilting my chin up. "I'm sorry."

"I feel bad," I say. "Seeing Luke's parents so upset, knowing this is going to crush Luke." I shake my head and ask, "Don't you feel bad at all?"

His blue eyes tell me he does. Jax may be cocky, but he's not an asshole. He draws a deep breath and says, "I'm not going to feel bad about loving you."

That's not exactly what I asked him, but my heart melts just the same. His arms slide around my waist, holding me close, his nose buried in my hair. It's a hug. He's hugged me before, lots of times, but this is the first time I've ever really felt the emotion behind it.

He's got me. We're in this together.

Tilting my head up, I whisper, "I'm not going to feel bad about this, either." Then I plant a soft kiss on his lips.

"Or this," he says, leaning into my neck.

"And definitely not this," I say, kissing him deeper.

CHAPTER TWELVE

JAX

SKYLAR WAS RIGHT. A kiss does say a lot, and this one is telling me in no uncertain terms that she's ready for more. Taking a step back, her eyes lock on mine. Without taking my eyes off her, I reach down, finding the remote to lower the shades on the windows. I won't share her.

Suddenly, it feels like we might only get this day. Before she has to decide about her business, before she has to decide about Chicago, before Luke finds out about us—this may be the last day of our holiday before the unknown descends upon us.

Skylar feels it, too, her body crashing into mine. There are definitely Gentleman's Rules for sex, the most important of which is, if you're only thinking about yourself, you're a selfish douchebag.

Gentleman's Rule—Number one priority in the bedroom is your woman, not your cock.

If you're with a real woman, her number one priority is you, so you don't need to be a prick. I'm in good hands with Skylar, who already has me stripped out of my t-shirt. Time to play catch up, so I rip her shirt over her head.

I only briefly saw her naked before and didn't get the opportunity to touch her or really admire her, but ever the gentleman, I should let her go first. Slipping my hands underneath her waistband, I kneel, taking her shorts and panties with me. On my knees, I look up at her, convinced she is the most beautiful woman I've ever seen, her skin without a tan line, perfectly smooth, her tits begging to be kissed.

"Turn," I say.

Her cheeks flush, but she slowly turns around, and as promised, I plant a kiss on her ass cheek. She giggles, the best sound, and I get to my feet, wrapping my arms around her from behind. I find the spot on her neck that I know makes her go weak in the knees. She moans my name, and I slip one hand down her flat stomach between her legs. Her body bucks at the contact. Gently, I nibble the lobe of her ear, whispering, "This is mine." My finger slips inside her, and her muscles clench. For me, this is just a warm-up.

Want to know what goes through a man's mind when he's having sex? For most men, it's logistics like "don't come too soon!" or "do I have a condom?" For me, right now, it's how fucking lucky I am to finally be close to her.

She turns, forcing my hand to her hip. Our tongues wrestle with each other. Her hand on my chest, she pushes me to the bed, straddling me. I can feel her heat even through my shorts. My cock thumps, wanting nothing more than to be inside of her, but he's not in control here.

Taking hold of her wrists, I force her to her back, pinning her arms over her head with one of my hands. If sex were a sport, I'd be the one in charge, the play caller, and right now, we are not in a hurry-up offense. It's time to slow things down. The goal isn't a quick score. It's multiple scores. And it's full contact.

She smiles shyly, and I gently kiss her lips, my tongue slowly stroking hers. My hand drifts higher, and for a second, I feel like a kid getting ready to cop a feel for the first time. I can't tell you why men are fascinated by tits, but we just are. In general, a woman's body is just more fun. Our dicks aren't nearly as entertaining as a woman's ass, tits, pussy—well, pretty much her anything.

She fits perfectly in my hand. She moans my name, and I lower my head, pulling her nipple between my teeth. Her back arches up as pleasure shoots through her body. Honest to God, I could stay in her cleavage all fucking day, kissing, sucking, biting. Maybe another day, right now my destination is a little lower.

Her body trembles as I kiss a path down her stomach to her belly button. Her fingers slip through my hair. There is nothing like a woman's hands in your hair as you go down on her. I look up, and what a view it is—her tits, a subtle bite on her bottom lip waiting for me. My only goal is to make her feel good—in oral, in bed, in every part of her life.

As soon as she feels my breath, her legs tense then fall open, inviting me in. One swipe of my tongue and one of her hands flies to the sheets, grabbing it tight. Her other hand stays in my hair, a gentle encouragement, but I don't need any. My hands on her thighs, I force her legs wider.

I don't consider myself a selfish man, but when it comes to her, I'm as greedy as they come. I devour her, slipping my tongue deep inside her, feeling her clenching around me, desperate to orgasm. She will come, but only when I'm ready. Massaging her inner thighs with my hands, forcing the lips of her pussy to open and close, my tongue flicks her clit.

"Oh, fuck," she cries out.

She's a sensitive little thing. It almost feels like a battle of wills—hers to come, and mine to make this last as long as possible. I can't help the grin on my face. This is the best Christmas Eve. Skylar and I used to play together during the holidays, showing each other our new toys. I much prefer to play with her like this.

No toys necessary.

The only playmate she needs is me.

Hoisting her thighs to my shoulders, I deepen my kiss, and she goes flying over the edge, calling out my name. Kissing her through her tremors, she comes down from her orgasm gently, her body falling limp. I look up at her, her eyes closed, a sweet, satisfied smile on her lips.

She opens her eyes, catching me staring and motioning with her hands for me to come to her. I slide up her body, kissing my way back to her lips. Her leg goes to my hip, and before I know what's happening, she hooks her toe under the waistband of my shorts, yanking them down.

That's a cool trick.

Our naked bodies mold together like they are two pieces of the same clay. Lightly, I brush some hair from her face, and she cups my cheek in her hand. Her leg winds around my waist, her heat beckoning me. God, I love this woman, every damn thing about her. I glide my dick inside her, our eyes locked on each other. I know in this moment, she is the last woman I will ever be with like this. Does she feel that good? Hell yes! But it's so much more than that.

Slipping myself in and out, her hands slide down my back to my ass. I am completely hers. All my power, all my strength, everything we use to define ourselves as men is hers for the taking. The gentleman rules, but the lady commands.

The cardinal rule of the gentleman's handbook is this—a man's purpose is a woman.

It's why we work hard. It's why we have children. It's why we do most everything in our lives. It's all for women. We may have muscles and brawn, but women yield more power in their pinkie fingers than we could ever dream of.

You may think you're the exception to the rule, but it's only because you haven't met your woman. The one that will bring you to your knees. The one that will make your life make sense. The one that you will break all the rules for.

"Right there," she moans, her nails digging into my ass. "Don't stop doing that."

Quick tip ladies, we love it when you talk to us. Lets us know we are on the right track.

Willing myself not to finish, not wanting to miss the moment her orgasm rips through her, I pound into her harder, making sure to hit just the right spot. Her grip on my ass gets tighter, her back starts to arch.

"Let me hear it, baby," I groan, not wanting her to hold anything back from me. A few more hard thrusts, and she screams out my name, her body coiling around mine tightly. Not taking a second to recover from her pleasure, she slips me out of her, rolling over, tilting her perfect, round ass in the air.

Christ, I love her, and not just the fact that she thought to let me take her from behind, although that doesn't hurt. I give her ass a hearty smack before slipping my dick back inside her. A woman's ass is a piece of perfection, and Skylar's is a fucking work of art. She knows how to work it, too, forcing herself back on me as I thrust into her. Taking hold of her hips, I encourage her.

"Fuck, you're beautiful," I groan through clenched teeth.

There's nothing better than watching my hard cock slip in and out of her wet pussy over and over again, as her ass pounds against me, my balls slapping against her clit.

She reaches between her legs, and just when I think she's going to touch herself, she gives my balls a gentle tug, ripping my orgasm from me. "Holy fuck!"

We collapse onto the bed, me beside her. Waiting for my breathing to return to normal, my fingers lightly roam the delicate curves of her body. Leaning up on my elbow, I see her smile, her dimple popping out, and I know it's more than sexual satisfaction.

She's happy.

I make her happy, and that's the best Christmas gift I've ever gotten.

***

THE DAY AND night roll together too quickly. The food gets delivered. The gifts get wrapped, but mostly Skylar and I stayed wrapped up in each other. We don't step foot outside all of Christmas Eve. We don't make it to church. We don't do anything except be together. This day has been a lifetime in the making, and nothing is going to get in the way of her being wrapped in my arms.

At midnight, I whisper "Merry Christmas" into her hair as she cuddles into my side on the sofa in front of the Christmas tree.

"Mmm," she moans, doing a little seductive stretch.

"Want your gift?" I ask, getting her attention.

She lifts her head, biting her bottom lip. "I don't have anything for you."

Is she kidding me? She gave me her. I'm good for the rest of my life.

"My gift to you isn't big or anything."

She smiles, her head tilting. "Tomorrow night," she says. "After everyone leaves. Give it to me then."

"Why then?" I ask.

"So Christmas lasts," she says. "I want it to last as long as possible."

I have to wonder if she's talking about the holiday, or me and her.

CHAPTER THIRTEEN

SKYLAR

It's Christmas, and I glance across the den at Jax. He's got Parker and Harper on the floor playing with a train set he bought for them. Malcolm's got his hand on Maci's belly, I'm sure talking about how next Christmas they'll have a new baby. Their parents are here, eating, drinking, and being merry. Jax talked to his mom today, and I talked to her, too.

I'm sure she sensed something was up between the two of us, but neither one of us let on. My mom came over before everyone else, and we got to catch up. Jax gave her the most beautiful handmade afghan, knowing her symptoms always worsen when it's cold. I have no idea where he found it. I can't imagine him shopping for something like that, but it doesn't look cheap. If that's his idea of "not a big gift," I may be in trouble.

Jax flashes me a smile, and I know what he's thinking. I'm thinking the same thing. When is everyone going to leave so we can get back to bed? I still can't believe we slept together. I always suspected that Jax would be amazing in bed, but I had no clue how amazing. It's not the multiple orgasms or his seemingly limitless stamina, although that doesn't hurt. It's the in-between parts. That's the part I didn't expect. How sweet he is. How close he holds me. How much it all means to him. I knew sleeping with him would be fun, that's a given, but I had no idea how much it would mean—to both of us.

While at least half the room knows about Jax and me, we aren't on public display. I sneak another glance his way. He's got a kid on each knee. He looks like he's having just as much fun as they are playing with the train. Harper leans up and whispers something in Jax's ear.

"Harper and Parker have a song to sing," Jax says, getting to his feet and quieting down the room.

Maci goes to them, encouraging them to stand up straight, their matching pajamas making them look like they are catalogue models. Malcolm joked that he hopes they fall asleep on the car ride home and go straight to bed. Christmas is exhausting for parents, I guess.

Harper and Parker start a very out of tune version of the "Reindeer Pokey." It's basically the "Hokey Pokey" with deer parts, but that doesn't stop Maci from stealing the show and shaking all about. Everyone busts out laughing, and Maci eats it right up, grabbing her husband's hands and trying to get him in on the action.

"Good Lord, we have to help her," my mom laughs, moving her arms. Before I know it, the whole room is dancing, but it probably looks and sounds more like we are having some sort of psychiatric fit with Maci as our cult leader. Jax grabs me, twirling me around. Laughter fills the air. It's exactly what Christmas is about—being surrounded by good friends and family.

"Uncle Luke!" Harper and Parker both yell.

Luke!

My eyes fly to the front door as Luke stands in the open doorway.

Holy hell! What's he doing here? I'd have more expected to see Santa Claus drag his fat ass through the chimney than to find Luke walking through Jax's front door.

The twins both run to him. He bends down, hugging them, but his eyes are fixed on me. Jax, Maci, Malcolm, my mom, and I all freeze while everyone else surrounds him. Maci steps to my side, holding my hand tightly.

I knew at some point I'd have to see Luke again, but I thought it would be on my terms. I'm not prepared to deal with this right now. It's Christmas Day, after all. Last time I saw him, he was in my bed with another woman. The pain of that is still too fresh. I thought it had started to scab over, but he just tore it right open again.

Luke's eyes go to Maci then to Jax, anchoring me, one on each side, making their allegiance known. It's left to Malcolm to bridge the gap.

"What a surprise," Malcolm says. "We didn't know you were coming. Thought you would be in Paris."

"Changed my plans. Got in a few hours ago," Luke says. "Saw my parents and then . . ." He crosses the room to me. My body feels rigid and cold like a corpse, but my heart is thundering in my chest. "Came to get my girl," he says, dropping to one knee in front of me.

"Oh my God," Maci exhales next to me.

What the hell? Of all the proposal scenarios I dreamt up, this was never on my radar. This can't be happening. My heart is pounding too fast. I feel my legs wobble. Luke looks up at me, his blond hair looking like he hasn't slept in days, his eyes looking just as worn. He pulls out a tiny black box, revealing a massive, emerald cut diamond in a simple platinum setting. It's exactly what I once wanted. A few weeks ago, this would've been my dream come true. Does he really think he can propose after what he did?

"Skylar," Luke starts.

I feel Jax shift, unable to watch another man propose to me. "Luke, get up!" Jax barks.

"What the hell?" Luke snaps, getting to his feet.

I place my hands on Jax's chest, forcing him back. His muscles are like a wall. "You need to let me handle this."

"No fucking way am I . . ."

"Jax!" I say, warning him.

"Umm," Maci says, ushering her kids to their grandparents. "Could you take the kids home?"

With my eyes, I tell Jax to hold his spot and then I step back to Luke. "You can't just show up here with a ring, not after what you did."

"I'm sorry," Luke whispers, trying to take my hand, but I yank it away, my eyes darting to the kids. I want them out of earshot before this all goes down. My eyes go to my mom. I don't want her to hear what Luke did, either.

"Mom," I say. "Can I call you later?"

"Skylar," she begs quietly.

"Please, Mom," I say, my eyes filling up. Unable to deny me, she says her goodbyes, and Maci and Malcolm's parents offer to give her a ride home.

Quickly, everyone starts gathering their things. The Christmas festivities are clearly over. Maci bends down to hug the twins.

"That's a pretty ring," Harper says to Luke. "You gonna marry Aunt Skylar?"

"Hope so," Luke says, smiling at me.

"All right," Maci says, pushing them toward the door to her waiting parents, everyone else already in the car.

Parker's little nose wrinkles up, and he says, "She was kissing Uncle Jax."

No, no, no! Things were bad enough already, and now an innocent preschooler just unleashed more hell—on Christmas Day! My eyes dart to Jax. If he's shocked, he doesn't look it. In fact, he looks like he's happy the cat is out of the bag.

Luke is frozen, shell shocked, just staring at me. Maci shoves everyone out the door, leaving just the five of us. The way it was for so long.

It's silent. The only sound is my heart thundering against my chest. It's the longest minute of my life.

"Mistletoe or something, right?" Luke asks, his voice low, hopeful, trying to make sense of what Parker said, searching for a rational explanation. "He saw you guys under mistletoe?"

I could say yes and let him think that, but I'm not going to lie to him.

Maci and Malcolm step between Luke and me and Jax. I take a deep breath. I told Jax to let me handle this, and now I have to.

"No," I say.

The love that was in his eyes five seconds ago melts into pain.

"That's some sort of payback," Luke yells. "Screwing around with one of my best friends to get back at me."

"Luke," Jax barks, stepping closer.

I don't like that they are this close to one another. An arm's length isn't long enough when tempers are flaring.

"Fuck you, Jax!" Luke barks.

"This has nothing to do with you," I say to Luke.

"You can tell yourself that all you want," Luke says, rubbing his temples, pushing on his eyes. "Jesus, Skylar, I came here to apologize, to convince you to marry me, and instead you're . . ."

"Happy," I say simply.

"No," Luke says, grabbing my hand.

"Let go of her," Jax yells, coming at us, but Malcolm holds him off.

"I'm fine," I tell him, holding my hand up.

"You're a fucking shit friend, Jax," Luke snaps. "I trusted you. I think she's here in good hands. That you're watching out for her, and instead you take advantage of her."

"It wasn't like that," I say.

"Skylar is with me," Luke yells.

"Luke!" I cry.

"What?" Luke says. "He should know he's second choice."

"Stop it," I beg.

"It's okay, Skylar," Jax says coldly. "He's desperate."

"Desperate is taking my sloppy seconds," Luke says, a smug look on his face.

I see Jax's hand ball into a fist at his side. Despite what romance movies depict, there is nothing romantic about having two men fight over you, especially when those two men were once good friends.

"She told my parents there was still hope for us," Luke says, glaring at Jax. "You didn't know that, did you?"

"That's not what I said," I cry, my eyes flying to Jax.

How dare Luke twist a conversation he wasn't even present for! I was quiet when they asked about Luke and me getting back together.

His parents can think what they want, but that wasn't an admission by me. I simply didn't want to hurt them anymore.

"What Skylar and I have is special," Luke piles on.

"You don't have to do this, Luke," I say. "You don't have to rip each other apart. Please."

Malcolm reaches out a hand to Luke in a comforting way. "Hey, man, let's go outside and talk and cool off."

"Good idea," Maci says.

Luke ignores the invitation, and his eyes narrow at me. "And you, have you even had your period since we broke up? I mean, if you got pregnant, would you even know whose baby it was?"

All I see is red as Jax's fist lands in the middle of Luke's face, a crushing blow to his nose, forcing Luke to double over. I hear a scream and look at Maci, but then realize it's me. Malcolm pushes Jax back. Luke doesn't retaliate, though, probably because he knows it would be no contest—Jax would win easily.

This is what I was saying before, the difference between them: Luke is usually very rational while Jax is passion first, think later.

Maci runs to get a towel from the kitchen for Luke and hands it to him. Luke wipes the blood from his nose then looks at me with such sadness. All our history together can be seen in that one glance—childhood memories, first dates, all our years as a couple. How did it all come to this?

"I'm sorry," he says. "I didn't mean that."

"I know," I say, my heart breaking. I hate hurting someone, anyone, but especially someone who meant so much to me.

"Can we go somewhere alone?" Luke asks, wiping some more blood away.

I look at Jax. I shouldn't. I don't need his permission, but I don't want to hurt him, either.

"A lifetime of friendship. Ten years together," Luke says, tossing the blood-stained rag aside. "You can give me a few minutes. Just me and you."

"You don't owe him anything," Jax says, reaching for my hand.

"I know that," I say, but I walk away and out the back door with Luke.

His head hanging, Luke walks past the pool down to the beach. I follow a few steps behind him. His stride is long and slow. I keep waiting for him to stop, but he just keeps walking. The waves of the gulf seem louder, more forceful than ever, the darkness stretching farther for some reason. The only thing heavier than the sand on my feet is my heart. I look back toward Jax's house, seeing him standing at the window, Maci and Malcolm by his side.

"Luke," I say, causing him to stop walking.

He doesn't turn to face me. "How'd we get here?" he asks, and I know he's not referring to our location.

There's no easy answer to that question. I broke up with him because our relationship was going nowhere? He screwed another woman in my bed? I fell for Jax?

Does it really matter how we got here? This is where we find ourselves.

He steps closer to me, glancing up at the house. I hate the look in his eyes, unable to disguise the disgust he feels toward Jax. "I know you wouldn't have," he pauses unable to say the words. "If I hadn't slept with that other woman like I did . . ."

My heart tugs like it's trying to pull me back to him. "No, Luke."

His eyes well up as he draws a deep breath. "That's why I can forgive you."

I don't want his forgiveness. I didn't do anything wrong. Okay, maybe sleeping with one of his best friends wasn't my best choice, but that's the thing—I almost feel like I didn't *have* a choice. What I feel for Jax is so beyond my control at this point.

"Can you forgive me?" he asks.

Luke is offering me his forgiveness because he wants forgiveness in return. Does he really think things work that way? That forgiveness is tit-for-tat?

"Someday," I say.

"Skylar," Luke says, grabbing my hand and pulling me into his arms. I try to wiggle free, but he holds me tightly to him, whispering over and over again, "I'm sorry. God, I'm sorry."

When his voice cracks through his tears, I stop struggling. He takes my face in his hands, lowering his head to mine, tears running down his face. I don't know if I've ever seen a more sincere apology in my life. I truly do believe he's sorry for what he did, but I can't throw him a meaningless, "*It's okay.*"

It's not okay. It started me on this crazy journey, so I speak the truth. "Thank you."

His hands slide around my waist, pulling me tighter. There's still hope in him, his embrace, I can feel it.

"Come back to Chicago with me," he says. "I know we can work things out."

CHAPTER FOURTEEN

JAX

"Get out of my way, Maci!" I say as calmly as I can, having not forgotten that she's pregnant. She's blocking the door, preventing me from storming the beach. I can't exactly move her out of the way in her condition. Even from here, I see Skylar in Luke's arms.

"This isn't the way to handle this," Maci says, her voice calm. "If you go out there and hit Luke again, you know Skylar isn't going to forgive you." I look down into her eyes. "Think about it. You know her. You know she cares about Luke and doesn't want to see him hurt."

"You care about Luke, too," Malcolm says.

"Fuck!" I say, pulling at my hair.

Maci pats my arm. "You have to let Skylar decide what she needs."

"She won't go back with him," I say, almost like I'm ordering the universe not to let that happen.

"I hope not," Maci says.

My eyes widen in disbelief. I can't believe she'd say that. She sits down on the sofa, nodding toward another cushion for me to join her. Malcolm stays by the door, not trusting that I won't charge outside, I guess.

I can't sit, but I do step a little closer to the sofa. "The other day you didn't seem too supportive of me and Skylar."

"I was surprised," she says. "Look, if Skylar wants to be with you, then I'll support you guys whole-heartedly. If she goes back with Luke..." She looks toward her husband. "Obviously, they've discussed this before. "After what he did, it will be hard for me to swallow, but I'd try for Skylar."

Malcolm clears his throat, forcing my eyes to the door. Luke walks in. "Where's Skylar?" I ask.

"On the beach," Luke says then turns to Maci and Malcolm. "Would you mind leaving me and Jax alone for a minute? Skylar could probably use you guys right now."

Why would Skylar need them? Is she crying? Is she planning on leaving? Did she tell Luke to go to hell?

Malcolm looks to me, and I nod, then Maci takes my hand and whispers, "Don't fight with him."

I give her a little nod, not sure how convincing it is, but know I can hold my temper as long as Skylar's not here for him to upset. He can say whatever the hell he wants to me, but not her.

"You boys behave," Maci says, throwing Luke and I each a warning glance, then Malcolm leads her outside.

Luke and I stand glaring at each other. The thing to remember in this situation is that he was once my friend, one of my best friends. In fact, only a week ago, I would've still said he was a friend. He's hurt. I know that.

He puts his hand in his pocket, and I wonder if the ring is still in there or if it's now resting on Skylar's finger. What the hell kind of proposal was that? Clearly, he didn't think that one through. Perhaps he should've read the Gentleman's Rules on the subject.

I move toward the window, looking toward the beach. Maci and Malcolm are just reaching Skylar. Maci wraps her in a hug, and I know she's crying. It should be my arms comforting her.

"Why?" Luke asks. "I thought we were friends."

"We were," I say. "But Skylar is more. She means more."

"You're a selfish bastard," he says, waving his hand. "All your rules. The bro code. It's nothing but a crock of shit."

"Luke, I know you're pissed. I would be, too, if I were in your shoes, but nothing you can say is going to get to me."

He leans back a little. "Skylar coming back to Chicago will get to you."

"She wouldn't," I say quickly, not wanting him to know how much that would hurt. How much my heart is hurting at the mere mention of it.

He smiles, and it's the meanest I've ever seen him look. Clearly, I don't know Luke as well as I thought I did. "Maybe I'll make a few calls and let your publisher and a few social media outlets know that The Gentleman doesn't follow his own rules." He gets in my face again. "You see, I could ruin your career and take Skylar, and there's not a damn thing you can do about it."

I didn't expect him to threaten my livelihood. I also didn't expect the sucker punch to the gut that followed. It hurts like hell, but I don't double over, and I won't go down. I'm going to follow Maci's advice and not punch back. If I beat the shit out of him, Skylar's protective instincts will kick in, and she'll feel the need to take care of him. I don't want that, so instead I stare him down, my jaw set.

It's not unheard of for brothers or male friends to get into physical fights. Goes back to early history when men solved their conflict through fists, not words. That's part of the male DNA. It's also not unheard of that after the fight, everything returns to normal and the two men are cool with each other. But I don't think that's going to happen here, though.

"Luke, it doesn't have to be like this. Skylar doesn't want our friendship to . . ."

"You fucked my girlfriend," he yells. "The woman I love. You think we can still be friends after that? You're fucking delusional."

"I'm not the one who screwed another woman in Skylar's bed," I say.

This time when he lunges at me, I move out of the way, sending him slamming into an end table. The table is solid wood, so it fares better than Luke, who I'm sure is going to have one hell of a bruise on his leg.

"I tried to be rational about this," I say. "But come at me again, and I won't be so generous."

He's smart enough to realize he's out-matched and starts yelling at me instead. *Fucking prick. Asshole. Son of a bitch.*

After one or two curse words, they kind of lose their effect and all start to sound the same.

"Get the fuck out of my house," I bark.

"Stop it!" Skylar screams, with Maci and Malcolm standing behind her.

Luke and I have been so busy hurling insults at each other, we didn't notice Skylar open the door. She places her hands over her ears, tears rolling down her face. "Please stop this," she says to both of us, freezing us to our spots, her head shaking in obvious disgust at our behavior.

She looks back at Maci. They don't say a word, but Maci knows what she needs by that one glance. Maci looks to her husband. "Go upstairs and get Skylar's things."

"No," I say, stepping toward Skylar. "You can't leave."

"Look what I've done," she cries. "I should've stayed in Chicago instead of bringing all my crap here, ruining everyone's Christmas."

"I can get us on a plane back to Chicago tonight," Luke says.

Fuck, I hate his smug tone, but thankfully Skylar hates it, too.

"I'm not going to Chicago with you. I'm doing what I should've done to begin with. Going to Maci and Malcolm's house."

"Please, Skylar," I beg.

She peers up at me with those blue eyes of hers and softly says, "I need to go. I need some time, some space."

Time and space? Hasn't she had enough time? We've cared for each other since we were kids. Hasn't she had enough space? She's lived in Chicago for the past several years. Our time is now.

Luke steps beside me. Skylar glances between us. Is she trying to choose?

Maci places a hand on each of Skylar's shoulders, urging her to the front door. Luke steps in front of them in one last attempt, pulling the ring out.

"I bought this for you. I want you to have it," Luke says, taking hold of her hand.

The massive diamond shines so bright the damn thing looks like it's laughing at me. This is my fucking nightmare, watching the cool metal of the platinum hit her finger.

Skylar jerks back like she's been struck by lightning. "I only want one ring to ever go on that finger. The ring my husband gives me." She looks up into his eyes. "And that's not you."

"It won't be Jax, either," Luke says.

"Maybe not," Skylar says softly, not glancing my way.

She folds his fingers over the ring then lightly kisses his cheek, and without another glance at either one of us, walks to the front door.

Malcolm comes down the stairs with her bag. True to his nature, he doesn't say a word. Luke walks over to him. I can't hear what he's saying. I see Malcolm nod, then he gives me a look. What it means, I don't have a damn clue.

The door closes behind them, and Luke and I are left alone again, only this time the feeling in the room is very different. We aren't fighting over the same woman. We've both been left by her.

"You lost her," he says, comforting himself with the knowledge that even though he lost her, too, it wasn't to me.

"Not yet, I haven't," I say, knowing I'll fight for her, but having no idea how I'm going to do that.

"I thought the same thing," he says, staring down at the ring still in his hand.

I don't think it was until this moment that he truly realized and accepted that she's gone, out of his life, that it's truly over for them. It doesn't bring me any comfort to see it, either. The fear that I'm in the same boat makes any relief impossible.

"How do you handle it?" I ask.

He looks over at me, the hint of a smile on his face. This is the face of my friend. "Drink?"

Grinning, I shrug, "I could use a drink."

He nods in agreement, and I walk to the kitchen and grab a couple beers from the refrigerator. I pop open the caps, handing one to Luke, who takes a seat at the kitchen island.

I lean against the counter and survey the damage. Wrapping paper litters the floor. Glasses, plates, and food left from what was a great party now sit cold, unappetizing. Even my Sequoia Christmas tree looks a little droopy. Then there's my friend. His eyes are black and blue, which only make his nose look worse, but it's his broken heart that's more obvious. I wonder if I look as crushed as he does. Hell, I probably look worse.

He picks at the label of his beer bottle, taking a few long slugs. We've been drinking together since before we were legally allowed to drink, but we both know this is it—our last drink together.

I broke the commandment, and we both know there's no way our friendship can survive. That's why we made the rule in the first place, to protect our friendship, to guard against this moment. A woman should never come between two friends. That's what we said. We just didn't account for Skylar, for love, for the one woman you'd break any rule for.

I'm not going to fight with him anymore, but the truth is, Luke was never my competition. When it comes to Skylar, I'm the only person that ever got in my own way. "Paris?" I ask.

His lips in a tight line, he nods and says, "Yeah, thought Skylar would jump at the chance to live in France. I was wrong."

He downs the rest of his bottle then gets to his feet, ready to leave, ready to end our lifelong friendship. He pauses for a second then turns back to me. "Are you sorry at all?"

"I'll tell you the same thing I told Skylar. I'm not sorry about loving her. I'm not going to apologize for that. I am sorry that I had to hurt you to get to her."

He gives me a nod and walks out. Over twenty years of friendship ends over a bottle of beer and one lousy Christmas. I wonder if I'll ever see him again. I'd think we'd run into each other at some point. Waterscape is small, and his family still lives here. I'm assuming he'll still stay friends with Maci and Malcolm, so we're liable to cross paths. No matter what went down tonight, I wish him good things in his life. It's easier to do that now that I know those good things won't include Skylar.

Grabbing a trash sack, I start cleaning up, tossing in plastic plates, wrapping paper. The more I pick up, the harder I throw the things in. Skylar's been gone less than half an hour, and the place feels completely empty without her. How is that? My place isn't furnished, but when she was here, I didn't notice. It felt full—full of her laugh, her smile, her tears, the sound of her breathing when she sleeps, everything that makes her special. It was only a few days, but it was everything.

It's Christmas. Skylar in my bed this morning was the best gift I've ever received. I've never woken up with a woman on Christmas morning before, spent all Christmas Day with a woman. But if I don't do something fast, this could be the one and only Christmas we ever have together.

I've written books about break-ups. How to move on. How to fight for your woman. But I don't have a single rule about how much time is appropriate or how much space I have to give her.

Skylar didn't come with a manual. She asked for time and space. Guess that's what's on her Christmas list.

Christmas! Her gift! She told me to give it to her tonight after everyone left, and that's one rule I'm going to follow.

CHAPTER FIFTEEN

SKYLAR

After assuring Maci that I'm fine for the twentieth time, I shut the door to the spare bedroom I'll be sleeping in. It's the room I always stay in. It's painted a buttery yellow with a queen size bed and a soft white comforter. There's an attached bathroom, and Maci always has it stocked with anything I might need.

It's not huge, but probably bigger than some of those tiny houses they build on that show Luke and I used to watch. Seriously, who can live in two hundred and fifty square feet or less? I'll tell you who—the Unabomber. His shack was the original tiny house. Maybe he started the craze, but look at what happened to him.

Luke!

God, he looked crushed tonight. I think he really thought I'd accept his proposal. I hated to hurt him, but I know me turning him down isn't what ripped his heart into shreds. It was finding out about me and Jax.

When I walked in on Jax and Luke yelling and fighting, it was too much, too much guilt. I can only blame myself for that. I realized in that moment that I need some time. If I want this to work with Jax or with anyone else, I need to deal with some shit first. I don't want to carry it all into a new relationship. I need to have that good, cathartic cry I never allowed myself, to curse mankind. It's why I came here for Christmas in the first place. I have to allow myself time and space to do that.

I can't look for a dick to cure what ails me. Maybe that's what I did this week. No, I know that's not true. I wasn't using Jax to avoid dealing with my feelings. Although his dick did make me feel a whole lot better.

Maci knocks on the door again, peeking her head in. She's become my own personal mother hen, making hovering an art form. "You're never going to believe what I have!" Smiling, I wave her inside. She holds out a carton. "It's wine flavored ice cream!"

I bust out laughing. "No way!"

"Oh yes," she says. "We'll have that heartbreak cured in two seconds flat."

She hands me the whole carton and a spoon. She's a good friend. She pulls out a sack of cookies for her and her unborn baby. Sitting across from me on the bed, she silently waits. It's not like Maci to be quiet. She's loud, fun-loving, always talking, but tonight she just sits.

I take a bite of ice cream, then another, and another—with each bite, more tears fall. Wiping them in vain, I say, "It's Christmas. You should be with the twins and Malcolm."

"Please," she says, waving her hand. "Those little suckers woke us up at four o'clock this morning. They're fast asleep."

I laugh, but more tears come. Maci wraps her arms around me in a tight squeeze. "That was really bad tonight," I say.

"A shit storm," she says.

"You were right," I say. "What you said that day on the beach. Jax and I being together *is* selfish."

"Oh, Skylar," she says. "I should have never said that."

"It's true," I say. "It was selfish of me."

She leans back, brushing my hair aside. "Here's the thing. Sometimes it's okay to be selfish."

"Not if it hurts someone else," I counter.

"Even then," she says.

"Jax and I could've waited a little bit. Taken our time."

"Love doesn't wait," she says. "You should know that better than anyone. It just happens like a force of nature. Love is impatient."

"That's not what the Bible says," I tease.

Tossing another cookie in her mouth, she says, "That Bible part means we should be patient with those we love, but love itself... she's a demanding, high-maintenance bitch."

I can't help but laugh at her colorful description.

"Think about it. Love keeps you up at all hours. Gives you butterflies. It comes out of nowhere sometimes, and you have no control over it."

"So love is a bitch," I say. "Sounds about right to me."

Maci laughs, handing me a cookie to dip in my spiked ice cream. "Luke will be okay," she says. "He'll probably find himself some French model."

I wait for it—the sting. The sting that should come at the thought of Luke in a relationship with someone else, but there's nothing. Maybe the ice cream has frozen my heart? Or maybe I'm okay with him moving on. If I'm okay with him moving on, does that mean I'm ready to move on? Then why am I crying? Is it over losing Luke? Knowing the five of us will never all be friends again? Knowing I'm the cause of the death of Luke and Jax's friendship?

"Now, Jax is another story," Maci says. "Boy loves you something terrible."

"I don't think I can talk about it," I say, tearing up again. "Talk to me about something else. You never told me what Malcolm got you for Christmas."

She smiles and tells me about the completely impractical Burberry diaper bag he bought for her and the new watch she bought for him. Maci is my best friend. I know she and Malcolm have arguments, but they seem so settled, so sure. They always have.

"Stop looking at me like that," she says.

"Like what?"

"Like my life is perfect," she says. "Because it's not."

"Please! Your husband adores you. You have the cutest twins ever, and now you're pregnant with a third."

She looks down, tossing her cookie back in the sack. It must be serious. One should never waste a perfectly innocent cookie. "This baby wasn't planned," she whispers.

"So? What does it matter?"

"It matters because the twins are four. They will be in school next year. Which meant I was going to have more time to devote to our business, to having a career of my own, and now . . ." She breaks down, covering her face with her hands.

"Maci?" I say, patting her arm.

"I wasn't happy," she whispers with a little cry. "When I found out. That's why I didn't tell you."

"Malcolm?" I ask. "Was he happy?"

"Oh, he was thrilled," she says. "He has the big career. You know people refer to me as Malcolm's wife or the twins' mother? It's like I don't exist except as it relates to them. God, I sound like such a bitch."

"No, you don't."

"I'm happy about the baby now," she says. "It took some getting used to the idea, but I'm starting to get excited."

"Don't worry about the business," I say. "We'll figure something out."

"I hope so," Maci says, squeezing my hand. "I don't want to give it up."

"I'll move back here," I say, holding her eyes. "That should make things easier. Plus, I'll be close to my mom."

"And Jax," she says.

I don't respond to that, unless you count the sick feeling in my stomach and the ache in the middle of my chest. "This will be good for us. Heck, maybe we can get into natural bath products for babies."

Her entire face changes from worried to excited in two seconds flat. "That's a great idea," Maci says, grabbing her phone to make notes, her mind already kicking into gear. "And fun soaps for kids. The twins love to use that stuff in the bath, but it always seems to leave marks on the tub or glitter gets everywhere, and you have to clean when they're done. It's a pain."

Our minds spin with scents, textures, and packaging as we brainstorm ideas. What Maci thought was going to be the end of her career is maybe just turning out to be the beginning of something great. That's the best kind of ending. The kind that leads you to a new beginning.

Is life doing the same thing for me?

Part of my life with Luke ends, and life is leading me to a new beginning with Jax?

"Oh, I can't wait to tell Malcolm about our new plan," she says.

My heart tugs, wishing I had someone to tell. That's one of the best parts about being in a relationship, you have someone to share all your happiness with.

"I'm going to text him," she says.

"Isn't he just downstairs?" I ask.

She laughs and shrugs, "Yeah, he hates it when I text him from the house."

A few seconds later we hear the sound of his footsteps coming up the stairs, a soft knock, then he sticks his head in and asks, "What's the big news?"

"Come see," Maci says, waving him in. She starts talking at a speed that only Maci can. I can tell that Malcolm is trying to follow her stream of consciousness rant, nodding his head. She goes on for what seems like forever without even pausing for a breath. Before she turns blue, Malcolm places a hand down on his wife's shoulder, smiling. "I know we thought I'd probably need to stop working or cut way back, but . . ."

"Go for it," he says, bending down and kissing her on the forehead. "I'll support you whatever you want to do."

She leaps into his arms. God, they look happy, both smiling, wrapped in each other's arms. Maci does a little wiggle, and I can't help but smile. She plants a small kiss on Malcolm's cheek, saying, "Think I'll sleep in here with Skylar tonight."

"You don't need to do that," I say. "I'm fine." They both give me a look. "Okay, I'm not fine, but I'm going to polish off the rest of the cookies and ice cream then go to bed."

"You sure?" Maci asks.

I nod, and she heads toward the door, but Malcolm doesn't follow her. "Be there in a minute," he says to her.

She gives him a curious look before leaving. "Malcolm, you don't need to worry about me," I say.

His head shakes. "There's a gift for you under the tree downstairs."

"What gift?"

"When you're ready," he says then walks out the door. "Downstairs."

"Malcolm?" I whisper-shout, but he either doesn't hear me or ignores me.

My heart sinks, knowing Luke really wanted me to have that ring. He must have given it to Malcolm to give to me. I'm not anxious to face that, so I clear off the bed and go to brush my teeth. I'll face that in the morning. Toothbrush in hand, I walk to the bedroom door, peeking in the hallway. No, I'll never sleep if I see that ring again. So I walk back into the bathroom to finish up, the brush moving faster and faster against my teeth. My hairbrush moves with the same force, but I'm sure that whatever is down there can wait until the morning, until I've had some sleep.

Turning off the light, I crawl into bed. Two seconds later, I sit up.

I won't be able to sleep until I know for sure what's down there. If it is the ring, I'm not sure how I'll handle it. I won't keep it. I hate to make Malcolm or anyone else return it to Luke. God, I really hope I'm wrong about what's waiting for me.

Taking a deep breath, I tiptoe down the stairs, careful not to wake anyone. From the staircase, I can see the Christmas lights are still on, the white light drawing me into the den.

From the bottom of the stairs, I can see the back of the sofa, the fireplace, but not the tree. My legs stop moving. Today has been the worst, and I'm not sure my emotions can take much more. I turn, my hand on the banister to head back upstairs, but my curiosity gets the better of me.

Taking a deep breath, I walk to the opening that leads into the den, expecting to find a little box for a diamond ring. What I find is much bigger than a diamond, and way more valuable. It's not from Luke, but from Jax.

CHAPTER SIXTEEN

JAX

FROM MY CHAIR in the corner of the room, I watch Skylar standing in front of the tree. She has no idea I'm here. When I convinced Malcolm to let me leave Skylar's gift for her, I had to stay. I told Malcolm I'd be taking up residence until I win Skylar back. Plus, I had to see this moment. The moment she got her gift from me. It's been a long time coming.

She doesn't touch it. The only wrapping is a bow, so she doesn't have to open it to know what I got her. Her hand flies over her mouth, and she makes a noise that sounds like something between a cry and a laugh.

Sitting in front of the tree is a pink cruiser bike with a white wicker basket, a bigger version of the one she wanted when we were kids.

I've had it hidden behind some boxes in my garage since Skylar and I went shopping a few days ago. The night Skylar was mad at me, I attached the basket, making sure the tires were filled and it looked perfect. I watch her run her fingers across the seat, the handlebars, still not realizing that I'm here. "Skylar," I whisper, getting up from my chair.

She jumps slightly then turns to me, her hand over her chest. "What are you doing here?" she asks.

"You told me to give you your gift after the party," I say, smiling at her.

She bursts into tears. There's no other way to describe it. Okay, so not exactly the reaction I was hoping for, but I rush to her just the same. Her hands cling to my shirt as her head buries in my chest.

"I didn't want to cry anymore tonight," she sobs.

Holding her face in my hands, I use my thumbs to wipe away her tears. "It's always been you, Skylar. It always will be. I'm not leaving here until you come with me."

"Jax," she whispers. "This is . . . Thank you." She glances back at her gift. "Did you get yourself a neon green one?"

Grinning, I say, "They didn't have that color. I had to settle for blue." I take her hand. "Together. That's what you wanted, remember?"

She nods, and I take a breath. I've given a lot of speeches in my life, but this one needs to outdo all of them combined. This one determines the rest of my life. I need to make her understand how much I love her. I need her to let go of her guilt about Luke. I need to convince her that I'm the man for her.

I'm a smooth talker. Always have been. I can usually talk my way out of any situation, but it seems now all my charms have left me. All the bullshit, all the rules, all I am right now is a man in love with a woman.

She rescues me, placing her hands on my cheeks. That's what the right woman does for a man. She rescues you from your bullshit, your bachelor life, your past—whatever it is that holds you back.

"I love you, too, Jax," she says, smiling. "I didn't leave tonight because I don't love you, or didn't want to be with you. I left *because* I love you. And I'm not sure I'm ready for it."

The only plan I've got here is to make it impossible for her to leave, and the only way I know to do that is brute strength, and I'm not referring to physical strength, but strength of heart. "You have to be," I say. "I won't have it any other way."

She laughs a little, shaking her head at me. "You're either the love of my life or my biggest mistake."

"Probably both," I tease her.

"Jax," she says, playfully pushing my shoulder, but I take her in my arms.

"You are my biggest mistake," I say softly. "Not telling you how I felt all those years ago. Letting some stupid rule get in the way. I won't make the same mistake twice. You are the love of my life, and nothing is going to get in the way of that, not even you."

When that one dimple of hers pops out, I know I have her.

Gentleman's Rule—When you find the right woman, never let go.

CHAPTER SEVENTEEN
SIX MONTHS LATER

JAX

"It's a girl!"

Tears running down her face, I place a hard kiss on Skylar's lips. "A girl," she whispers.

I wipe her cheeks, wondering what her reaction will be when it's her own child being born, if she's this overjoyed at Malcolm and Maci's third.

"How's Maci?" Skylar asks.

Malcolm fills everyone in on the delivery, which was much easier than with the twins. The waiting room is filled with Malcolm and Maci's parents, other relatives, and friends—me, Skylar, and Luke included. He just happened to be in town when Maci went into labor.

Skylar and I hadn't seen him since Christmas Day. We were shocked to see him here today. It's been six months. Other than the polite smile they exchanged when he walked in, there's been no other contact. I know she hates that our relationship started off at Luke's expense, and I know she hates the awkward silence between them.

I shake Malcolm's hand, and Skylar gives him a huge hug. "When can we see Maci and . . ?"

"No name yet," he says. "Maci can't make up her mind. Grandparents first."

Another round of congratulations and the parade of visitors starts. Unfortunately, that removes some of the buffer between Luke and us. Skylar gives my hand a squeeze. "It's such a happy occasion,"

Skylar says. "Maybe . . ."

I'm not about to let her face that alone, so I stand by her side as we cross the room toward Luke, even though I know there's nothing that can really bridge the distance between us. I think Skylar knows that, too, but that doesn't stop her from trying.

"Luke," I say, stretching out my hand.

He stares down at it for a second. I feel the same way. It's weird to be in the same room after all this time, but I know this is important to Skylar.

He leaves me hanging, instead choosing to give me a nod. "Jax." Then his eyes land on Skylar. It's obvious she and I are still together, and the pain of that still resonates in his eyes. "I saw your new baby products in a store in Paris," he says softly.

Apparently even an ocean can't keep Skylar out of his life. She smiles, telling him about how well things are going for her and Maci and their business. I'm damn proud of her, and I can tell Luke is, too. At least we have that in common.

He still has a soft spot for Skylar. Maybe he always will. I, on the other hand, have become the one he blames, which is fine with me. As long as he's kind to Skylar in these awkward moments, then he can blame me all he wants.

"How's Paris?" Skylar asks.

It's the exact kind of inane, bullshit conversation I hate having, and it's sad that I'm doing it with one of my oldest friends. Still, I would do it all again to be where I am with Skylar. Career-wise, we are both doing well. The house finally got totally furnished, and Skylar moved back to Waterscape.

Crazy woman thought she was going to rent an apartment when she moved back. I asked her to move in with me, but she said no. So she stayed with me while she searched for a place. Six months later, she's still there. Her clothes are beside mine in the closet, her car is parked next to mine in the garage, and best of all, I wake up beside her in bed every morning. She's not going anywhere.

"Who's next?" Malcolm asks, coming into the waiting room,

eyeing the three of us. I'm sure he's hoping that we don't come to blows celebrating his daughter's birth.

"Go ahead," Skylar says, motioning to Luke.

"Thanks," he says, reaching out toward Skylar, but he pulls himself back. Some habits are hard to break. Another nod in my direction, and Luke disappears down the hospital corridor.

Malcolm turns to follow him, as Skylar calls out, "Malcolm, does Maci really not have a name?"

He exhales, stepping toward us. "She does."

"Is it something weird?" I ask.

He glances at Skylar, and I'm not sure why. Do they want to name the baby after her? "Maci wants to use your baby name?"

"What baby name?" I ask, my eyes flying to her stomach.

Skylar just shrugs her shoulders. "I'm not sure what she's talking about."

Malcolm wrings his hands together. He looks completely exhausted, and he's not the one who gave birth. "Sailor," he says. "Maci said that was always your name for your daughter one day."

Skylar's face blossoms into a huge smile. "When we were in preschool and played with dolls!"

"So you don't care if we name her Sailor?" Malcolm asks.

"No," Skylar says. "Of course not."

Relief floods Malcolm's face. "Maci loves the name but wouldn't use it because of you."

"She's a good friend," Skylar says with a smile. "It's fine. Go name your daughter."

He rushes out the door. Skylar shakes her head, and I wrap my arms around her waist. "Skylar and Sailor?" I ask, raising an eyebrow.

"It was cute when I was six!" she laughs.

"When we have a baby, we aren't naming him or her any of that weird shit. Nothing after a fruit or something you need a dictionary to pronounce," I say. Skylar's face has the strangest look. Her dimple is out, so I think she's happy, but her eyes look like I'm in trouble. "What?"

"When we have a baby," she says, repeating what I didn't realize I said.

Skylar pregnant with my baby? That's not a bad thought. Not at all. "I guess we should do the traditional thing and get married first," I tease.

"Probably so," she says with a laugh.

The Gentleman's Rules for getting engaged have changed over the years. I've recommended everything from well-thought-out proposals to spur-of-the-moment ones. I know that Skylar thought a lot about getting engaged in the past, so I have to top all of that. I have to do something that she won't expect. The truth is, I've been thinking a lot about how to ask her. Hell, I've been thinking about it since last Christmas. But there are only two words that I need to say.

"Marry me?" I ask, falling to one knee.

EPILOGUE

JAX

Gentleman's Rule for a wedding—Stay the hell out of the way!

"Five minutes," Malcolm says, slapping my shoulder. Maci has threatened him within an inch of his life if I'm late to my own wedding. She informed her husband that she was holding him personally responsible, so the poor guy is a nervous wreck.

Skylar is not the bridezilla in our wedding. It's Maci, who even with a newborn has taken it upon herself to handle most of the planning. Well, that's not entirely fair. She's taken it upon herself to make Skylar's wedding day everything Skylar wants it to be. Since Skylar's mom can't do a lot physically, Maci has been the go-between, making sure that everyone's vision is carried out.

I've got the honeymoon covered! Once Maci let it slip that she and Malcolm didn't have sex on their wedding night because they were too exhausted, I devised a plan. Wedding early in the day, so as not to interfere with the wedding night.

Maci informed me several times that six months was not long enough to plan a wedding, but there was no way we were going to postpone. Christmas is just a couple days away, and we'll be spending it on our honeymoon. Where exactly, only I know. I wanted to surprise Skylar. We're getting married on the anniversary of the day that I picked her up at the airport. Let's hope she doesn't throw up today like she did then.

"Ready?" Malcolm asks.

I nod, heading out to take my place at the altar. In just a few short minutes, I'll have a ring on my left hand. To some guys that symbolizes a life sentence, but I can't wait. I'm so fucking proud that's she's going to be my wife, there are no words.

We're getting married in a little chapel in Waterscape that overlooks the water. The church is covered in white irises. White petals are scattered on the floor. It almost looks like snow. The chapel is small, which is perfect for us. Malcolm is my best man, Maci is her matron of honor, and that's the entire wedding party except for Harper, Parker, and Sailor, who are serving as the flower girls and ring bearer.

I see Maci in the back of the chapel, encouraging Harper and Parker, who are pulling a little white wagon with their baby sister in it. Every person in the church collectively sighs, they're so damn cute. My mom winks at me from the front row, and I know she's thinking that I'm next for kids. All in good time!

The kids safely make it to the front, then Maci starts down the aisle. I look over at Malcolm next to me, a big smile on his face. I'm sure he's remembering when the roles were reversed, and I stood by his side when he married the love of his life. They were barely twenty-two at the time.

Of course, back then Luke was standing with us.

I'm sure he's aware that Skylar and I are getting married, but we haven't seen or heard from him since Sailor was born. I know he stays in touch with Malcolm.

Maci reaches the altar, and the music changes. It's the bride's turn. Everyone gets to their feet, blocking my view.

I step forward a little. The back doors open.

There she is.

All the air leaves my chest. She's standing there in a white lace gown, the sun shining behind her, picking up hints of silver in her dress. The dress is full at the bottom, and Skylar told me it had a long train, but it's the plunging neckline that has my full attention. Her brown hair is down in loose waves. Skylar looks beautiful every day, but right now she's beyond stunning. I can't believe she's really about to become my wife. I'm one hell of a lucky man.

I see her before she sees me, but when her blue eyes find mine, she smiles. She takes her first step toward me all alone. Her dad is gone, and her mom wasn't physically able to walk her down the aisle. The days leading up to the wedding, that weighed on both her and her mom. The aisle isn't wide enough for her wheelchair and Skylar's dress, and her mom refused to have her daughter roll her down the aisle. I know that made them both a little sad.

I'm not sure why I didn't think of it before, but it seems like the right thing to do now. I take a step down off the altar. There's a rustling in the crowd, unsure what's going on. Skylar pauses, too, but when I flash her a smile, she continues to walk toward me, her train trailing behind her.

Halfway down the aisle, I meet her, holding my arm out to escort her the rest of the way. She slips her hand into the crook of my arm. The diamonds of her engagement ring catch the light. I had it custom made for her. I can't tell you how many diamonds are on the thing. There's the center stone, and it's surrounded by smaller diamonds. It almost looks like a snowflake. One of a kind, just like the woman wearing it.

"Wow," I whisper, my eyes taking her in.

When she smiles, I forget myself and pull her to my lips, my hands landing on the bare flesh of her back. Not only is the dress low cut, but it has a completely open back. The crowd starts laughing.

"We aren't at that part yet," Skylar whispers, placing her hand on my chest.

"For you, I break all the rules."

ALSO BY PRESCOTT LANE

All My Life
To the Fall
Toying with Her
The Sex Bucket List
The Reason for Me
Stripped Raw
Layers of Her (a novella)
Wrapped in Lace
Quiet Angel
Perfectly Broken
First Position

ACKNOWLEDGEMENTS

For the past few years, I've sent holiday cards out to readers, but this year has gotten away from me, mostly because I was writing this little baby. So I hope everyone considers this book a Merry Christmas and Happy Holidays wish from me. 2018 has been wonderful—it brought my books *To the Fall* and *All My Life* into the world. And now this one.

The list of those to thank for this incredible year is too long to name. I wish I could list every person who has ever taken a chance on me, taken a chance to read an author they've never heard of. I wish I could hug all the readers and bloggers who have been with me since the beginning. Your loyalty and support mean more than you'll ever know.

Merry Christmas to my team—Nina Grinstead, Social Butterfly PR, Michele Catalano, Michelle Rodriquez, Nikki Rushbrook. You ladies keep me sane, go crazy with me when I need it, and stay by my side through thick and thin. Love you so very much.

I wish you all a safe and happy holiday season. May all your Christmas wishes come true!

Hugs and Happily Ever Afters,
Prescott Lane

ABOUT THE AUTHOR

PRESCOTT LANE is originally from Little Rock, Arkansas, and graduated from Centenary College in 1997 with a degree in sociology. She went on to Tulane University to receive her MSW in 1998, after which she worked with developmentally delayed and disabled children. She currently lives in New Orleans with her husband, two children, and two dogs.

Contact her at any of the following:
www.authorprescottlane.com
facebook.com/PrescottLane1
twitter.com/prescottlane1
instagram.com/prescottlane1
pinterest.com/PrescottLane1

Made in the USA
Columbia, SC
30 December 2022